# SHARDS
## OF
# RAIN

MATHIAS G.B. COLWELL

# SHARDS OF RAIN

MATHIAS G.B. COLWELL

*For Michelle, I love you.*

## CHAPTER ONE

She was being followed. Of that much Abby was certain. Although, who it was and why they were following her was still unknown.

Rain —real, actual rain—came down in sheets, soaking through her overcoat and seeping into her boots. Riddled with holes, the boots were almost worn out. She'd have to steal another pair soon. Or trade for them. But Abby didn't have anything left to trade, or at least, nothing she was willing to give away. She pulled her coat tighter and tried to ignore how wet her socks were. The annoyance of being damp and cold paled in comparison with the fact that someone was stalking her in the grey afternoon light. The rain was a bad omen. Too much noise in the background could be a distraction—and that was dangerous.

Abby chanced a careful glance over her shoulder, masking the movement as best she could, so as not to alert her follower to the fact that she was aware of his presence. As soon as he knew she was onto him, the stealthy pursuit from a distance would likely be over, and the real chase would begin. Or was it them? A chill ran through her at the thought of multiple pursuers. She hoped it wouldn't come to that. Maybe she could still give him the slip—although the streets weren't nearly crowded enough to make that likely. The city was dull today. The red tile, greenish copper roofs, and varicolored buildings all somehow managed to look grey in the cold. People were staying inside, like any sane person would. As she should. If only she'd had someplace safe and *inside* in which to stay. Somewhere her stalker hadn't sniffed out.

She'd first realized she was being pursued a week ago, in what felt like another time, when the worst she'd had to fear was hunger, cold, and the occasional night prowler stumbling upon one of her haunts.

But then it had *happened.*

It had been an accident, but somehow, someone had found out. They must have seen it. Someone must have shared that knowledge, and she hadn't been safe since. They were chasing her now, and they wouldn't stop. She was too valuable. She'd have to get as far from here as possible, go somewhere beyond their grasp, where nobody knew what had happened. Then she might be safe. But leaving in and of itself was difficult enough. There was no point to leaving the city until she gained some distance. Why leave if her shadows were still close enough to continue their pursuit?

Abby pictured a beach. An island. A warm sunny day to contrast the water that sluiced down from the sky. At least it was water that was falling. The other options were far worse.

She shook her head, drenched hair clinging to her face instead of retaining its usual curly, springy volume. Thoughts like that would get her caught. She had to get away, and then never do it again. No matter what. Maybe if it never happened again nobody would come after her.

But they were after her now, and there was no avoiding that fact. Abby felt the creeping of panic begin to rise in her chest.

She looked over her shoulder again, and this time he saw her. She'd grown careless. Their eyes met, and she knew she had to run. Abby took off at a sprint, cobblestones slippery beneath her worn boot soles—worn so much that nearly all the tread was gone. Glass crunched beneath her boots as well, a familiar sound.

Breath coming in panting gasps, Abby looked back again, all pretense gone, all need for secrecy over. The man behind her was running also, and he was much faster.

*Damn, these boots!* she thought. And damn the fact that she'd barely had more than a meal a day for the last half year on the streets. It had made her weak.

She whimpered involuntarily as she ran and hated herself just a little bit for making that sound. She could hear him now, his feet pounding rhythmically behind hers, somehow managing to sound louder than all the rain in her ears. Blank stares, scared stares met her gaze as she glanced at the people on the main street.

Nobody stopped for her. Abby didn't shout for help.

This city wasn't that kind of place. This wasn't that type of world.

At least, not anymore.

She ducked into an alley, and then dodged into another one, hoping that somehow, she could lose her pursuer in the narrow, twisted warren. She took another and another turn in quick succession, blindly, hoping to find freedom and escape.

What would he do if he caught her? Not knowing her fate if she were caught was almost worse than being chased.

The latest blind turn was a dead end. Not because the street ended, but, because the narrow alley was clogged with fallen construction materials. Some project had fallen—scaffolding, beams, materials and all had been left to ruin. It blocked the way. She could try and worm her way through but not quickly enough to get away. He was too close behind.

Typical. Fallen construction in a world fallen to pieces.

She turned, still breathing hard from the run. Her follower had slowed to a walk, a predatory prowl as he covered the last few yards between them. Hands raised high to show her he meant no harm. So, he was going to take her in in one piece then. Or was it a trap?

Tears formed at the corners of her eyes as terror took over. People taken for doing what she did—being what she *was*, she was forced to admit—didn't come back. Or at least, they weren't the same if they did.

"I'm not going to hurt you," the man said slowly and carefully, the way a person would speak to a wounded animal to keep it from spooking. His blond hair and beard were as soaked as she was. Black jacket, black pants, black boots. He was a study in darkness. In fear.

"So, I can just go then?" she managed to quip somehow, despite the gnawing terror.

The man chuckled darkly. "No, I'm afraid not. We both know that isn't happening." He spoke with the accent of this place, but his English was good. Almost like he'd spent time in the Federation of the Isles, where Abby had grown up. Before it had dissolved.

He took a few steps closer, and Abby reflexively shuffled back a step until her back pressed against rotted wood from the clogged street full of construction.

The bearded man tilted his head slightly and spread his hands wide this time. "There is nowhere to go. Come quietly, it will be easier on you."

Abby responded by pulling a knife from her pocket, the one real weapon she possessed. It was a longish, rough piece of glass, with cloth and twine wrapped around the base. Makeshift, but it had cost her all the rations she'd had at the time to trade for it. His eyes narrowed in response. Not in wariness, but in annoyance. Like a fly to swat, rather than a dog about whose bite he needed to worry.

He *tsked*. "Now, now, none of that, girl. No need for pain."

The implication that there would be pain sent a chill down her spine and made her struggle to swallow. But one thing she'd learned on the streets was that you never quit fighting.

She gripped the hilt tighter.

The blond man closed the distance, carefully but quickly until he was only a couple feet away. The last step between them evaporated in a heartbeat as the man moved so fast, she couldn't even react. He grasped her wrist and twisted, and the blade fell from her hand immediately. She stifled a scream and tried to wriggle free and strike him, but he grabbed her other

5

arm in his other hand. She squirmed, but he was a big man, and even stronger than he looked.

*It's over*, she thought bitterly. *I barely even put up a fight.*

A sound paused their struggle. Abby heard it at the same time as the man. The faint whine of something falling, which turned into a screaming rush as the object careened toward the earth, closer and closer, directly at them. The man swore in his native language and tensed to move, but it was too late. They were dead.

The giant shard of glass screeching toward them through the rainy sky was huge, about the size of a car. If Abby had felt terror before, the prospect of now certain death practically squeezed the breath from her lungs and held her heart in a vice. But there was nothing they could do. It was too late.

It wasn't fair, Abby thought in some strange, detached moment. She wasn't ready. And to think, she'd have to die with this bear of a man's hot breath on her face.

*No!*

Her mind rejected that thought. Her soul screamed and raged at existence for a tortured, wild instant before her broken will, her being, snapped together like an iron rod. No. Not like this. Not now.

Abby willed the universe to hear her, as she wailed and shrieked internally. And it did. It listened. And it *happened* again.

Time froze.

A frigid moment, cold from some kind of empty void that only she could move in and out of. She'd done it again. No time to think. It wouldn't last long. It had been only momentary the first time—a few meager seconds—the last time it had *happened*.

The bearded man hadn't moved since the universe had answered her. The silence stretched as the immense blade of glass hung suspended a few yards above their heads.

Frantically, Abby wrenched herself from the man's powerful grasp. She felt her control, whatever little bit she possessed in this void, shred and fray at the edges. She didn't have much time. It would end soon, her frozen moment would die, and she with it.

Abby pulled herself free and dove to the side of the alley, through the wet, and as time unfroze around her, she raised her arms to shield her face from the debris she knew was coming.

The glass finished its course from the heavens and cleaved a portion of the bearded man from the rest of his body, before shattering and sending sprays of smaller shards all around the narrow alley. Her arms took the brunt of the damage from the splintering bits of glass, and luckily her coat was thick enough to protect her.

The silence that followed was filled with rain, filled with reality, a silence filled with sound—not like the frozen moment of existence that had saved her life.

She'd done it again.

"Pauser," the man spat out the bubbling, bloody word. The title. Somehow, he was clinging to life, one arm, one leg, and part of his torso shorn from his body.

"You'll never tell," she taunted, rediscovering her spirit despite the fear she felt at what he'd just called her.

"You bitch! You Pauser bitch!" He raged with his last

breaths at the girl who'd saved herself instead of helping him. The light faded from his eyes, and his angry visage was the only lasting imprint of life on his face, made all the more eerie for the vacant eyes he now possessed.

Abby swallowed. She eyed the man for a moment longer before bending to retrieve her fallen knife. Leaving him behind her in the alley, she walked nervously, not because of leaving a dead body—people were accustomed to the occasional death from Sky-Shattering, as they called it—but rather because if there had been one person sent to hunt her down, then there would be others. She had to stay sharp and on guard. At least until she was far away. Maybe all the way across the Atlantic would be far enough. She clung to that hope. It would have to sustain her.

But for now, something more mundane would have to do, something to take her mind off of what she was and what she was capable of doing. A meal. And a place to sleep.

The rain began to slack off, almost in response to her wishes for food and shelter. It wasn't exactly what she had wished for, but it would do. Slowing to a drizzle, the water falling from the sky was far more pleasant than the alternatives.

# CHAPTER TWO

THE CITY-STATE OF PRAGUE WAS SUBDUED. IT WAS A DRAB evening in early autumn, not cold enough yet to merit overcoats and scarves, but a few sprinkles spotted the railing of the balcony that looked out over the Vltava River. The castle on the hill rose on the near horizon. Though it had stood practically unused for centuries, it was populated now. Prague had a king again—well, petty warlord was more like it—as did many cities in the world. The balcony door was open wide, and a mild chill pervaded the room, a cold left over from the rain this afternoon. Just enough that most people would stand up and close the door.

He didn't move. He didn't feel the lack of heat. He was warm from the whiskey that screamed through his veins. Jonathan David Dean looked at the bottle knocked onto its side on the polished wooden table. His handgun lay near it. A Walther—practically a relic these days. A pool of brown liquor was splattered across the table after spilling from the bottle's mouth. Jack Daniels. Imported from what had once been Tennessee, from the region under Nashville's control. Nashville was a City-State now, just like Prague. Much like most of the world. At least, the parts of it he'd seen. Time-Warfare had seen to that.

Here in Prague other drinks were preferred, but to someone who'd been raised in the American Federation, the whiskey was one of the only reminders of home he could manage to get.

He heard a faint sound of revelry from the old town square. Barely enough to pierce the grey atmosphere. Most of Prague lay silent. He stared out the double doors on his balcony and watched the river slide by. It was dark ash, charcoal to the grey of the sky. He spun the bottle. A tiny spray of whiskey droplets flicked across the table as the bottle spun loosely on its side. A few of those brown droplets flecked his white dress shirt and navy-blue suit jacket that hung open at his chest. He leaned back slightly and spun the empty Jack Daniels bottle again. It whirled on its axis in a mesmerizing fashion. Jonathan felt his face go slack as he stared. The bottle whirled and whirled, until it slowed; slowed like the earth would one day slow in its revolution around the sun, when the universe like all things, gradually came to its end.

He lifted the glass of whiskey—all that was left from a nearly full bottle—and held it wearily against his face. He left it there for a moment before finally taking a sip. The cool of the glass against his flushed cheek was almost as satisfying as the drink itself. He sipped again, this time more deeply, and felt the familiar burn, the sourness in his mouth already predicting tomorrow's hangover.

Tonight had been close. Much too close. J.D.—his mind flitted between the numerous aliases and various versions of his name that he had used over the years—tried to care. He tried to care that tonight had almost been the end. He nearly managed to. Operatives from somewhere, some feudal state governed by the newly minted king of this, or the freshly inaugurated president of that region, had somehow made him —had realized what he was, what he'd been, and tried to kill him. He'd been sloppy. He was too used to Prague. It felt too much like home. He'd been there almost two years now. Ever since the PACK fell. Ever since he'd realized there was nowhere for him to return to.

He lifted the glass again and took another sip. The door clicked behind him and instantly, despite the booze, his gun was in his hand and ready to fire. He spun around lithely, if a trifle unsteadily, to face the door.

J.D. was at his most dangerous when there was a hint of whiskey on his breath. Perhaps not at his best, but his most dangerous, certainly. The gun was remarkably steady in his hand considering how much whiskey he'd just consumed. His tolerance was rising. He made a mental note to cut back. He knew too much alcohol wasn't good for a person—especially in his line of work—just like he knew he would ignore the mental note.

The door creaked slowly open and a hand reached through to wave in a harmless fashion. A voice sounded through the door.

"J.D., you gave me a key for a reason. Put down the gun."

J.D. hefted the Walther in his hand so that he held the shaft instead of the handle, placed it back on the table, and slumped into his chair.

"Come in, Sigmund. How did you know I had the gun in my hand? I know you didn't see me," J.D. said.

A short, thin young man with glasses appeared through the doorway, walked over to the table, and sat in a free chair. "I know you, J.D. I didn't have to see you to know you had a gun trained on the door. Your instincts are to shoot first and ask questions later."

"Well, you'd forgive me the snap judgment if you knew the kind of day I've had."

The thin, pale young man brushed a hand nervously through his brown hair that was just shaggy enough to need cutting, but short enough that it had yet to fall over his eyes. He pursed his lips.

"J.D., you know I hate it when you call me Sigmund. The name's a hand-me-down from some ancestor whose parents were infatuated with a famous psychologist a long time ago."

J.D. waved a hand and made a face to say the complaint was unimportant. "Right, sorry. Siggy."

Siggy shot him an annoyed look. "You might understand what it's like to care about a name, if you weren't parading across New Central Europe using a different moniker every night." New Central Europe was what this region was now called, though it was more of a geographical term than any implication of alliance.

"I am not parading," J.D. retorted with a slight slur. He

spun the bottle again idly and another spray of droplets stained his clothes.

"Fine, gallivanting. How about that?"

J.D. rolled his eyes. "Siggy, you're so dramatic. Always exaggerating. I was here in Prague all day and the day before that as well. In fact, I was in Berlin only for a few nights and then Warsaw, and before that I was here. This is home, after all. A de facto home, but home all the same. At least for now."

Siggy ignored the jab. "Is that a bullet hole in your jacket?"

J.D. glanced down and saw the ragged tear in his coat. "Why, so it is. I told you, you wouldn't believe the absolutely dreadful day I've had. And by dreadful day, I mean the fact that I ruined my favorite suit."

"It's not your best suit," Siggy disagreed. "The black one is better."

"I didn't say this was my best suit, I said it was my favorite. It was my lucky suit. Not anymore, I guess." J.D. frowned as he let the flap of his jacket fall against his side. He reclined in his chair again, feeling the front two legs tip precariously off the ground.

"Maybe it still is. You're still alive, after all." Siggy raised his eyebrows and the glasses moved on his face.

J.D. made a thoughtful face. "So I am." He sipped his drink again, savoring the last of his whiskey. He'd have to find an importer who owed him a favor soon. This had been his last bottle, and now that the PACK was finished, J.D.'s finances had mostly dried up. He traded on favors as much as physical currency these days.

"Do you have what I need?" he asked Siggy.

"No." Siggy hunched his shoulders. "You see, what happened is—"

J.D. cut him off. "I don't want to hear it. You know me? Well, I know you. You're lazy." The flatness in his voice made Siggy shrink for a moment, but just as quickly the little man rose up, haughtily.

"Now look here, Wolf. Being a genius slacker, a genius underachiever, used to take real guts. It used to fly in the face of societal standards. It was a badge of honor. A point of pride. But not now. The world burned and everyone's motivation burned with it. It takes all the fun out of slacking when brilliant shopkeepers and factory workers are a dime a dozen."

"Your point?"

Siggy grimaced. "My point is that I'm not lazy. Lazy is boring and cliché now. I'd never go in for cliché."

J.D. peered at Siggy disbelievingly. Siggy had a habit of coming up short. He also had a habit of coming through for J.D. in the most important of moments. It was a crapshoot which Siggy you were going to get. All he could do was hope for the best and pray to whatever God existed that Siggy was on his game.

"If you say so, Siggy. And I'm not a Wolf anymore. No one is. The Wolves disappeared when the PACK ended."

PACK. The Pacific-Atlantic Conflict Keepers. First the old-world countries had broken up, forming new and loosely allied federations all over the planet. That had lasted, and still did last in many places. Then the larger federations had risen up, banded together, and joined PACK—global governance's last gasp before the federations finally began to dissolve into the current City-States. It was a new world—again. The PACK was gone now that the rest of the old-world governing system was gone. Dissolved after their short, decade-long reign as resident world-conflict controllers and general behind-the-scenes manipulators. The PACK had essentially pulled the strings worldwide, determining which conflicts were snuffed out or avoided and which ones were allowed to occur.

"I really am sorry I couldn't get what you wanted," Siggy said, exuding genuine contrition. "I tried, but I couldn't get through the firewall."

J.D. waved a hand. "Maybe it's for the best." He shrugged with a tired sigh. "It was a mission from an organization that doesn't even exist anymore."

"You have to move on at some point," Siggy agreed, before continuing, "but in case you're not sure, I'll keep working on it." He pulled an oversized laptop out of a ragged leather bag.

"On that note, I'm going to go for a stroll. Clear my head a bit."

Siggy shook his head in disbelief. "Only you would brave Sky-Shatter and go outside just to clear your head. You know people die just walking around out there." People only went outside when they had business—things to do, places to be. Random falling shards of glass-like substance could make you reevaluate your priorities.

J.D. shrugged again. He stood a tad woozily and stuffed his Walther down the back of his pants before pulling the flap of his jacket over it. He pulled a black overcoat over his bullet-ridden suit and exited his third-floor apartment quietly. Siggy was already at work, seeking some way to electronically extricate the information J.D. needed.

The sky had turned almost to night and the late evening air was a shock of reality to the booze-fueled brooding he'd been doing. He shook his head side to side the way a canine shakes water from his fur coat, hoping to clear his head even further.

J.D. walked without purpose for a time, taking turn after turn, weaving his way through the red roofed heart of Prague. Tile roofs met centuries-old architecture painted in a variety of colors. He could see the spires of the various churches and towers stabbing the twilight sky, hinting at a darker, more ominous past than they truly possessed. It was all run down. Prague, like most City-States he'd visited, seemed to care just a bit less about its people than the old countries had once done. Politicians were more like feudal warlords these days, interested only in power and in what they needed to do to get and keep it.

Broken glass crunched under his feet, the way it did everywhere in the world. A decade or so ago, the Solar Shell had begun to break and shards of the formerly protective glass covering now regularly threatened to skewer those who braved the open air. He kept his ears sharply tuned to hear the faint tinkling of falling glass, the only warning a person ever got that it was time to hightail it and find cover. People like him, out for whatever reason, moved in a muted hush, the mannerisms of people attuned to the air, to listening for any sound of danger. Inside you could be as loud as you wanted, but outside, it paid to be quiet and vigilant.

The greatest technological and architectural feat in all of

history, and it had failed in stunning fashion, becoming responsible for as many deaths as it had prevented. Over the last century and a half, holes in the ozone layer had begun appearing, first over sections of the southern hemisphere, but soon enough gaps had begun appearing all over the world. Sun exposure became a real worry, and doctors and scientists and all the so-called experts began predicting mass cancer outbreaks in the not-so-distant future if something was not done about it—not to mention the general temperature increase and climate shifts. And so, the world leaders of the time had pooled their resources and set about to fixing the problem. From inception to completion the Solar Shell was viewed as a near miraculous creation. Almost divine in nature. J.D. remembered the first time someone had explained it to him as a child.

"Imagine a bubble, Jonathan, the way it's round and clear. And imagine sunglasses. The way they shade your eyes from the sun." J.D.'s father's voice pierced through the years, and for a moment, he was back in the American Federation, in the Virginia Territory. "Now imagine you put that bubble and those sunglasses together. You combined them. That bubble could now protect anything inside of it from sun damage, don't you think?"

J.D. had nodded vigorously to his father, trying to maintain the charade that he understood. At the time it hadn't made any sense. But he'd fooled his father and his father had continued speaking. "Well, son, that's essentially what the scientists of the world have done for us. Great minds, great people, got together and found a way to build a bubble around the earth—

way high above the clouds—and put in protective glass to prevent sun damage." Wonder colored the way his father had explained the Solar Shell, even when describing it in the most basic and general terms, the only way a 7-year-old child could hope to understand such a complex subject. Yet to this day, it was still the easiest explanation for J.D. to understand. Science and the technology weren't really his forte. That was more Siggy's area of expertise.

He continued walking through the night, keeping his ears peeled for any sound of falling glass. Over the years it had become clear that the Solar Shell was exposed to harsher elements and pressures and corroded more quickly than originally expected. It began breaking and falling in small slivers and chunks. Not enough to fully compromise its intended function, but enough to make a person pay attention to the sky. After all, it only took a very small piece of glass to kill you if it fell from high enough. Though, every once in a while, those chunks of glass were much larger than one might expect. J.D. had actually seen a piece of glass the size of a storefront hit the ground outside of Dublin once, back when he'd still been reporting to headquarters.

J.D. breathed deeply and enjoyed the brisk air. A few passersby walked the streets as well. As he neared the old town square the crowds thickened somewhat. Revelers out early for the night's entertainment, moving quickly between locations until they could make their way indoors to the safety of an establishment. People had grown more cautious, but life didn't stop just because it had grown more dangerous.

J.D. circled the square once, keeping his attention sharp,

letting the last of his drunken haze lift from his mind. His feet began to find their way back through the city center and toward the river again, toward home, when suddenly he felt the familiar and too-contrived bump of a body colliding with his back. He spun around one hand already behind his back, ready to draw his weapon.

# CHAPTER THREE

HE FROZE. IT WAS JUST A GIRL. MID TO LATE TEENS, MAYBE. Not short, but not tall either. Dirty, dark brown ringlets that looked like they hadn't been washed in weeks were still stuck to her face from the earlier rain. Sharp brown eyes peered at him from a slightly hollow face that was only a couple shades lighter than her hair. Hollow like a person who had spent months eating just enough not to starve. Yet somehow, despite her ragged appearance and her unwashed, underfed body, she managed to be beautiful.

"Sorry," she mumbled and turned away quickly, ready to melt into the crowd that was present in the square.

Quick as he could, his hand flashed out and grasped her wrist. "Not so fast," he said with deliberate precision.

The change in her visage was alarming as he pulled her back toward him. Vulnerable, weak eyes and a scared face transformed into the face of a small, panicked beast, cornered and about to be caught.

With one hand still grasping her wrist, J.D. held the other hand out. "Give it back."

Fear turned to a sullen, burning anger and intelligence, carefully concealed but still apparent in her doe-eyes. She didn't fight—she was smart enough not to do that—instead, she wordlessly handed back to him the few bills of money and coins she'd pulled from his pocket and wadded into her grimy hand. They weren't even worth much these days. Currency was only as good as the system controlling it, and right now, the City-States across New Central Europe changed leaders like a dog traded fleas. That instability didn't help the economy. Barter was better than coin in most instances. But some people were desperate for anything.

"Let me go," she said with an air of hostility. It was half a statement and half a question.

J.D. released her wrist. As he did, he saw the sharp shrewdness reappear. She was just about to disappear again when he spoke.

"Are you hungry?" He wasn't even sure why he asked.

The word hungry seemed to give her pause. Almost against her will, he could see his words reel her in. She turned back toward him warily.

"That's a rather stupid question."

"It is?" he asked mildly, suddenly feeling a buzzing echo from all the whiskey he'd drunk. Perhaps he wasn't quite as sober as he'd thought. A small smile formed unwarranted on his lips.

"Yes," she answered.

"Yes, you're hungry, or yes, it's a stupid question?"

"Both," she said flatly.

"If you tell me why it's a stupid question, I'll see to it that you aren't hungry for a good while. How does that sound?"

Greedy curiosity bloomed on her face and was just as quickly squashed and replaced by the bitter mask she kept.

"It was a foolish question coming from you."

"Coming from me?" he prompted her further.

She nodded. "I know what you are—realized it as soon as you turned around. Even most average people could look at me and figure out enough about me to guess that I'm hungry, especially if they caught me picking pockets. But maybe not all, maybe the most unobservant wouldn't. But you're different. I know what you are." Again, a look of fear crept back into her eyes.

"And what do you think I am?" he asked softly, almost gently.

"A Wolf," she whispered. Wolf. A label based on the acronym of his prior affiliation.

He stared at her for a long moment. "Thank you for speaking that quietly. It'd be worth my life if you'd have said that louder. We weren't well loved in these parts." He glanced at a few people staring suspiciously at them. "But, you're only half right. I *was* a Wolf. But I'm not now. The PACK doesn't exist anymore."

"If you aren't a Wolf anymore, then why are you carrying that?" She pointed to the small bulge at the back of his pants.

"Just because I'm not an agent anymore doesn't mean I'm not dangerous." He winked at her.

His charm didn't elicit any reaction. They stared at each

other for another long moment, and he really looked at her this time. He had thought she was in her mid-teens, but now he was reevaluating. She was thin and had a lithe look about her, contributing to her youthful appearance. But she clearly had a keen mind and some wit to accompany it. And she was tightly controlling the fear he saw roiling behind her eyes. Maybe late teens. Nineteen maybe? Her clothes were a tattered assortment. She wore tight black pants with some holes in the knees, a navy t-shirt that hugged her form, and a black jacket that hung open and unbuttoned.

"So, how about that food I promised you?" he volunteered cheerfully.

"If you want to feed me, why don't you just give me that money?" she rebutted.

He *tsked* in the way that always annoyed Siggy. "I can't very well reward you with money for a failed pickpocketing attempt, now can I? And anyway, half these places would prefer to barter, and I don't think you'd be inclined to give what they'd be asking."

She winced slightly in response to his statement. No, she wasn't the type to be giving out those kinds of favors in reward for food. No wonder she was so hungry looking. But she shook her head with the exact annoyance he knew his remark about her failure would elicit. She took a thoughtful step backward, weighing her options.

J.D. pressed on, "Besides, how am I supposed to pick up another bottle of alcohol on the way home if I give you all my money now? I have run out of whiskey—yes, I know, a terrible tragedy—and simply must have some more of something, and soon." So much for cutting back.

"So how do you plan on feeding me?" She stopped moving and asked, the wariness still in her eyes and on her voice.

"You see, there's this thing called cooking. Have you ever heard of it? It's a rather strange occurrence where you combine cold ingredients over something hot and thereby make food."

She almost cracked a smile, but quickly regained her composure. "You must be crazy to think I'll come with you. I just met you."

J.D. shrugged. "Your choice, I guess. But you've already figured out what I am—what I was—and what I'm trained to do. If I wanted to cause you harm, I could've done it already and been long gone before anyone around us was any wiser." He motioned to the dull flow of people meandering around them, like a stream passing a pair of stones.

He could see hunger warring with caution in her eyes. As it often did, hunger won.

"Alright, but I warn you, I have a knife." Belatedly, she seemed to realize how flimsy her bravado sounded and blushed. J.D. had the courtesy not to say anything. He just motioned for her to walk alongside him. She did, but with enough space to bolt if the need arose.

They walked in silence, stopping only for J.D. to buy the bottle of alcohol he mentioned. Not Jack Daniels, unfortunately. They were too far from the former American Federation to come by that brand very easily. Glass crunched under his dress shoes and under her once-durable black boots. Suddenly, a noise from afar reached his ears, like the old wind chimes his grandmother had put up all around the house back in Virginia Territory. A faint tinkling, an almost magic sound. That sound meant possible death now. He grabbed the girl and spun her hard against a building, shielding her body against the wall with his. Hopefully, there was enough of a lip on this building to protect them. The angry sound of indignation died in her throat as she saw the shower of glass from the heavens crash into the cobblestoned streets where they had just been standing. A few flecks of glass rebounded, and J.D. felt them pepper the back of his legs, but the rebound had none of the stealthy ferocity of the shards that had rained from the sky.

She was breathing hard, her mouth sending hot air onto his neck. He pulled back slightly from her. A look of fear was supplanted by a look that could only be described as wonder as she looked from the glass on the street to his face.

He expected her to cry or show some sort of fear at their near-death experience, or perhaps get angry at him for manhandling her. Instead, she smiled, the first smile he'd seen from her.

"I don't think we know each other well enough for you to be holding me this close," she murmured jokingly, placing a hand on his arm.

J.D. stepped back and cleared his throat more awkwardly than he normally would. "Right. Of course. By the way, I'm J.D."

She looked at him for a moment, searching his eyes for something. He didn't know whether or not she found it. "Abigail. But I mostly go by Abby."

They reached the apartment soon after and climbed the

stairs to the third floor. He stuck the key in and unlocked the door. As they stepped in, Siggy was still sitting hunched over his computer.

"Nothing yet, J.D.," He said with his back still to them. At the sound of multiple footsteps Siggy spun around and paused. "And I see you've brought a guest?" His inflection rose in curiosity.

"Abigail, Sigmund. Sigmund, Abigail."

Abby nodded at him from a safe distance away.

"He's harmless, I promise," J.D. said and made his way to the kitchen.

"I prefer Siggy," Siggy said, flashing an annoyed look at J.D.

Abby mirrored the look. "And I prefer Abby."

They turned their annoyed stares toward J.D.

He decided to sidestep the issue and get to more important matters. "Right then. Supper?"

# CHAPTER FOUR

"So how'd you peg me for an agent—or ex-agent, that is—from just a few moment's interaction with me?" J.D. asked, speaking through a mouthful of stew. Potatoes, carrots, and some kind of meat. Abby hoped it was chicken, or at least something familiar. People ate all kinds of things these days. And it was worse on the street. She'd yet to give in and eat roasted rat the way other waifs she encountered had, but it had been a near thing at times. Whatever this stew was, it tasted good. Abby hadn't had anything quite this good in weeks.

"What, like it's hard to tell?" she quipped, wiping a bit of greasy sauce from the corner of her mouth with her sleeve.

J.D. just rolled his eyes. Abby looked at the other, younger man, across the wooden table. He was quite a bit younger than the agent, only about five years older than herself—well, perhaps a few more than that—but he looked young. She supposed it was the mop of hair, or the glasses, or maybe it was just the overall pleasantness of his face that seemed to speak of innocence and youth. Sigmund—Siggy, he'd said—Siggy stayed silent, watching their interaction, not volunteering much. He looked kind and innocent, but he ate with the determination of someone who'd spent time on the street himself. It wasn't that uncommon really. Warlords rose and fell, and the turmoil their machinations created left people exposed to all kinds of difficulties and challenges. Winding up on the street when your building changed hands was far from an uncommon tale.

"Come on, seriously, how'd you know?"

Abby shrugged at J.D. again. "Just intuition I guess, legacy of a misspent youth."

"Ah," J.D. said quietly, and Abby hated the pity she heard in his all-too-knowing voice. It was part of the reason she hadn't answered directly in the first place.

"What?" she muttered, shoveling another bite into her mouth and glaring across the table at her rescuer from earlier in the evening.

"Yes, do explain. Please," Siggy agreed, speaking with the accent of Prague on his lips. Here they were, three people from three different places in the world, sharing a meal together like old friends. It was actually fairly uncommon, in Abby's experience. Not just the sharing part—she found people to be singularly selfish—but the geographical variety they represented. Former American Federation, former Federation of the Isles, and New Central Europe all in one place. Not only were they from different places, but they all sounded different, with Abby rounding them out with her accent hailing from Dublin.

J.D. glanced at Abby before sighing and then beginning to speak carefully, making a too obvious effort not to look at Abby as he spoke. "I'm guessing her parents were PACK," he began, focusing on Siggy, "and judging by the state of her dress and the fact that she was wandering the streets of Prague looking to pick pockets, I'd say they're probably dead." He said the last bit gently, finally glancing her way, but those words couldn't be sugar coated. It had only been a couple of years. The pain was still fairly fresh.

She swallowed back the agony of the memory. "Not too shabby, mate," Abby declared with as much nonchalance as she could muster. The pity in their eyes told her that it hadn't been enough to hide the truth.

"If it's any consolation, my parents are dead, too," Siggy volunteered with a sad smile.

J.D. cleared his throat. "Mine, too."

Abby just shook her head in annoyance. "Well it's not. Misery doesn't negate misery." She softened her tone. "Look at us, just a few orphans sitting at the same table."

"It's been long enough for me that I'm starting to forget the details," J.D. murmured, looking almost surprised he'd volunteered that bit of information. *How old is he?* Abby wondered.

"Well, this is entirely too morbid," Abby declared. "This is the first insulated building I've spent any time in for the last month, and I'm certainly not going to waste it talking about my dead family. Didn't you buy some alcohol?" She focused her attention on J.D. who was finishing his bowl of stew. "Seeing as I was kind enough to return your money—"

"—was caught and forced to hand it back over."

"—that bottle is by right at least partially mine. How about a nip?" She raised her dark eyebrows.

J.D. rolled his eyes again good-naturedly. "Well, you just make yourself at home, don't you?" But he stood up, walked to a painted white shelf on the wall in the kitchen and pulled out the bottle. Trade was more localized, things coming from afar difficult to come by. The clear liquid—likely some type of vodka—wasn't something J.D. would likely have grown up with in the American Federation, but it was better than nothing. Abby had spent time all over before her parents had died, so she wasn't picky.

Abby grabbed the bottle from the center of the table where J.D. had set it, along with a few small glasses. She'd finished her bowl of stew a long time ago, and was eyeing the pot longingly, while the two of them were still working on theirs, but for now the drink would have to do.

She poured each of them a drink, slid them their way, causing tiny spills to leave a track on the table. J.D. rolled his eyes at her for the third time. She wondered if he'd ever stop doing that.

Abby picked up the glass and lifted it. "To the dead, may we not speak of them again—at least not tonight."

Siggy and J.D. looked at each other, shrugged and lifted their glasses and mumbled something sounding like agreement. "To the dead!"

They tilted their shots back at the same time Abby did. The fiery liquid slid down her throat and burned with a warming fire. She didn't exactly love the taste, but she'd grown accustomed to it over the last couple of years. Sometimes street folk had some, and a drink or two could help stave off the cold. Or at least it made you feel it less, even if the danger of the elements didn't actually wane.

Glasses empty, she quirked her hand for the two of them to slide them back her way. They obliged. She began the process of filling them again.

"Have some more, why don't you?" J.D. said with a smirk.

Abby shrugged. "One thing you learn on the street, don't say no to anything free, and take as much as people will possibly give you."

That got a wry chuckle from J.D. and an uncomfortable laugh from Siggy. She slid the glasses back their way again.

They tipped them back again. "Another?" This time Abby asked.

"Not for me," Siggy gasped. His had evidently gone down the wrong way.

"I can keep going as long as you can," J.D. said with a bit of a challenge in his voice.

"You don't need any more either, you had nearly an entire bottle only a few hours ago!" Siggy exclaimed.

"Stop exaggerating, Sigmund."

"Siggy," Siggy mumbled, already sounding tipsy after just two drinks.

So, a drunk. Abby pondered what that might mean, whether it made her safer or not. She looked J.D. in the eyes as the two of them tipped back the third successive drink. This one hit her quickly, and she felt it before it had sat in her stomach more than thirty seconds.

It was rash to drink this much in such a short time with complete strangers. What had possibly possessed her to do such a thing? She was already growing lightheaded.

"So, agents?" J.D. cocked his head at her.

"Hmm?"

"Your parents were in PACK. Were they operatives, then?"

Abby let out a disgusted breath. "Did you seriously not listen to my toast a couple minutes ago?"

J.D. made a face of complete unconcern. "You're drinking my drink and eating my food, least you could do is give me answers."

She made a noise in her throat, whether it was anger or agreement, she wasn't even sure. She made a face and responded. "No. Not agents. Ambassadors."

His eyes opened wide.

"What?" Siggy asked again, ruddy cheeked.

"Idealists," J.D. answered. "Means her parents were probably true believers as they were working to spread the PACK's influence in an increasingly hostile environment. No other reason to put yourself and your family at such risk. By the end, the PACK was hated pretty much everywhere other than home turf. Nobody likes to feel like they're being controlled, and whatever you believe to be their motives, there's no denying that the PACK was aiming to do just that."

All of a sudden, Abby couldn't stand to be even a hint sober if they were going to have this conversation. She poured a fourth drink, although she sipped it instead of throwing it back. She lifted the glass in affirmative response to the ex-agent's remarks.

"Nail. Head. You," she muttered bitterly. "Fat lot of good it did them, too."

"We all die someday." J.D. shrugged, a picture of nonchalance.

"How utterly poetic," Abby replied bitingly.

"It's all those Time Warfare fanatics' fault," Siggy mumbled. Had two drinks really got to him so quickly? Maybe he was younger than she thought. "If it weren't for those damn Turners and Pausers, the world probably would have gone on the way it was."

Abby froze, but neither of them even glanced her way as the subject was broached.

J.D. waved his hand in dismissal. "They just accelerated the decline, but it was already happening. The first half of the 21st century was punctuated by dispute after dispute until the world hung perpetually on the brink of mass warfare. Disputes over religion, over resources, over old alliances that didn't even matter any longer. It was tinder waiting to catch. The first Pauser was just the spark."

Abby listened as intently as she could through the roaring in her veins. Stupid to drink so much, and yet she hadn't been so full or warm for a very long time. She hadn't felt this safe since her parents had died.

J.D. sipped another drink of his own and dipped his spoon into his bowl for the final bite, continuing to pontificate despite the mouthful of food. "Time Warfare just gave every local wannabe despot the opportunity to either settle old scores or gain resources. Until the chaos ensured everything broke down. There were decades of madness before the PACK arose. It was short-lived, and probably flawed, but not a bad idea as a whole." He tipped his head in Abby's direction. Did he think she cared one bit about the aims of a ruined organization, just because her parents had died for it?

Well, maybe she did. But only the tiniest bit.

He must've too; he'd worked the PACK, after all.

"What do you mean?" she asked.

J.D. shrugged. "World peace, central rule, and so on and so forth," he said as he waggled his hand expressively, wobbling his head a little as he did. "Leaders and rulers worldwide were getting assassinated left and right for years before the PACK was created. All it took was one Pauser stopping time and sticking a knife in somebody to settle an old score, or one Turner rolling back time by a minute to play out an assassination attempt and see how body guards reacted before replaying it again a moment later, with full foreknowledge, to set the world ablaze. Everyone and anyone could be a target. And every petty criminal and government official—often there's not much difference between the two—fancied himself a warlord all of a sudden. It was mayhem...or so I've been told."

"Well?" Siggy asked.

"Well what?"

"Aren't you going to tell us why PACK was a good idea at its core?"

"I don't know if I'd go so far as to say it was a *good idea,*" J.D. backpedaled slightly, "but I understood its aim. A more peaceful world. Problem was, after decades of Time Warfare, all the petty little tyrants had gotten too big a taste of freedom to relinquish it again. PACK sprung up but within ten years it was broken again, facing resistance from nearly all sides. Short-lived." He finished bitterly. Abby figured he must have at least believed in the organization somewhat to work for it and speak of it so.

"What's your take on Time Warfare?" Abby asked suddenly. Was it the drink making her this bold—no, *reckless*?

J.D. snorted. "Stay as far clear of that lot as you can. Nothing but trouble. A warlord will stop at nothing to get their hands on a Pauser or Turner, and if they can't control them, they'll kill them for fear of who else they might be working for."

Abby swallowed. It wasn't exactly disdain for what they— what she—was. Rather, it was a harsh practicality. She shouldn't care what he thought. She'd felt similarly until not too long ago when she first realized what she was.

J.D. continued, alcohol keeping his tongue loose. "Yes, Alojz—the warlord here in Prague—would want a Time Fighter even more badly than he wants me."

"You?" Abby frowned.

"You see a drunk, washed up agent," Siggy said somberly on behalf of his friend, "but as you both said earlier, his skill set was enough to save your life tonight. I know it's saved mine before. The warlord here in Prague could certainly make use of it."

"Why thank you, my good sir," J.D. bowed over the table from a sitting position as best he could, tipping an invisible cap mockingly. Siggy snickered slightly and then they both started laughing like buffoons. There was a real camaraderie here.

They were true friends. It was something she hadn't seen in years. The streets could be unkind. They fostered distrust between people, not friendship.

"Seriously though, what are you going to do about the warlord? He won't take no for an answer forever." Siggy swallowed nervously as he looked at J.D.

"He'll just have to develop patience, now won't he?" J.D. smirked. "It is a virtue after all. Or so I've heard."

Siggy opened his mouth to retort, no doubt something sincere and worried—Abby was already beginning to see the dynamic here, and there was no doubt that Siggy was the worrier between the two, with J.D. being the reckless one—but the crash of the door exploding inward and a body somersaulting inside startled them all, sending them jumping to their feet, bowls and glasses clattering in the commotion.

Abby was astounded to see that despite how much J.D. had drunk throughout the course of the day, the ex-agent already had a steady gun in his hand.

Before she could take in anything else, shots were fired from multiple directions.

Abby screamed and the world froze.

# CHAPTER FIVE

J.D. STOOD ON ONE SIDE OF THE TABLE, LEANING UP AGAINST it, gun aimed at the man who had burst in through the doorway. In a split second, he catalogued information as he'd been trained to do: short hair, unshaven face, muscular body, charcoal grey clothing from top to bottom, stare of lethal concentration as the man honed in on J.D. as the danger in the room, just as J.D. zeroed in on him.

Was today finally the day? Fates knew he probably deserved it. Nobody was an operative for any length of time before he accumulated a long list of sins to atone for. And they were in such close quarters. He heard the man's gun fire a shot. Too close. He'd never dodge this one, there wasn't enough time.

J.D. pulled the trigger. He felt his gun kick, felt the bullet leave. And then—

Suddenly, he was across the room, near the sink, with Abby

crouched over top of him as if she'd tackled him. J.D. shook his head to clear the confusion and lifted the terrified girl off of him, her face mirroring Siggy's across the room. Both were younger than he was, and likely hadn't seen violence the way he had.

What had happened?

J.D. assessed the room carefully. The man lay dead on the floor, blood pooling underneath him from an exit wound in his back, sightless eyes gazing at the cracked ceiling. A bullet hole was embedded in the wall directly behind where J.D. had been standing. The bullet should have hit him.

But then again, he should have been halfway across the room. It was a small kitchen and dining area, but still, he hadn't moved on his own.

J.D. cast a cautious look at the girl, as an idea began to formulate. But she had been across the table from him, how had she managed to tackle him? Dishes and utensils were scattered as if someone had frantically clawed their way over the top of the table in an effort to reach him.

"You saved my life." He said the words quietly, narrowing his eyes at her.

She shook her head mutely. Terrified. Of him?

She should be.

"No sense denying it, Abby, there's no other explanation for how we came to be here, when we were just over there." J.D. pointed back across the kitchen toward the table.

"No," she mumbled, avoiding his eyes, desperately clinging to the denial. Her hair was almost fully dry now, and her curls were no longer plastered against the side of her light brown face but had regained some of their springy full volume. She clutched a crude glass knife she'd no doubt made or bartered for on the streets as she stared at the dead man. People all over had begun fashioning tools, weapons, even artwork out of the fallen glass. When the heavens gave you something free, why not make use of it?

Siggy seemed to be clueing in. "You were here. Now you're there. You should be dead. How is that possible?"

"You saved my life," J.D. said again softly. "Might as well fess up to it. I owe you one. Besides, this isn't the first stretch of time I've been missing. I was a Wolf for long enough to come across a few of you."

He watched her visibly try to pull herself together. "Well, even if I did, I was just returning the favor from earlier." Some of the snap was back in her voice, but her eyes were still on the floor.

Finally, she met his gaze. "You can't tell anyone."

"Pauser?" Siggy directed the question towards Abby a bit breathlessly. He had always been easily excitable.

Reluctantly she nodded. "It's new. I've only done it a couple times before this."

"And judging by the length of time and your need to tackle me, you're still figuring it out. You haven't been able to stop time for long, have you?"

She shook her head. "It's usually been for barely more than a few seconds. This time was maybe five seconds, barely enough time to get to you."

"Well, I'm glad you did." J.D. flashed her a pearly grin. "Only question now is who is this man, and what did he want? I can't believe Alojz is that desperate to take me out yet. I've only said no to him twice."

J.D. walked over to inspect the man. A fairly nondescript appearance. Typical for some of the best operatives J.D. had faced, the kind of people who often hired themselves out to warlords and other rulers of the various City States around the world who needed muscle, or who needed a fine instrument of killing but couldn't get their hands on a Time Fighter.

Time Fighter. That was what she was. He'd known it minutes ago, but the name drove the point home. Another thought crept into the back of his mind. As if she could read his mind, Abby spoke up.

"He wasn't after you. He was after me. I was almost caught by another one of them, earlier today. But a glass shard saved me. I paused then too, only way I was able to get out of the impact zone."

"You're being followed," J.D. stated flatly, swinging an ominous gaze her way. The girl seemed to shrink before him at the tone and the look on his face. "You didn't think to tell me that when you accepted my invitation for a meal? Not even after you realized who and what I used to be?"

"Easy now, J.D., she's just a girl. Take it easy." Siggy had walked over and put a calming hand on his shoulder. "Besides, you said it yourself. She just saved your life."

"It's entirely different to save a person's life from a danger of your own making," J.D. grumbled, but Siggy's words had yanked him back from the precipice of his anger. The girl was looking sufficiently guilty anyway. No need to pile it on.

J.D. sighed. "How old are you anyway?" He put a hand on his forehead to think. Then walked over to the messy table, righted the bottle of vodka that had spilled most of its contents, and poured himself the last bit left in the bottle. He swallowed it quickly.

"I'm nineteen," Abby responded to his back.

He froze. "Shit, you're hardly more than a kid." He was speaking to himself more than to anyone else, but she huffed slightly at his description. Siggy was right, she was just a girl.

"And how old are you?" Abby snapped.

"Don't worry about me," J.D. shut her down. And the look on his face must have conveyed his annoyance with her because she bit off the retort on her lips. He had to think. What on earth had he gotten himself mixed up in?

———

Abby looked at J.D. with a mix of emotions. Should she feel guilty for dragging him into this? The old her would have said yes in a heartbeat. The new survivalist version of herself that had lived alone on the streets these past years didn't exactly agree. When you saw an opportunity, you took it. When someone came along who could help you, then you didn't spurn the help—even if they hadn't exactly offered you aid outright.

"What?" the ex-agent muttered grumpily, as if he could just sense her looking at him. He was still staring at the dead body in the entryway. The doorway was at one end of the small dining and kitchen area. The apartment had a balcony—tiny as it was—but the rest of the unit was fairly modest.

"Do we need to do something about him?" Abby asked. She wasn't entirely sure what to do with a dead body in a house. On the street, she would have just left him and moved on, without a second thought.

"Yes."

Abby waited for J.D. to elaborate, but he didn't volunteer any more information.

"Well, aren't we worried about someone showing up to investigate the disturbance?"

This time it was Siggy who turned her way. The younger man raised an eyebrow. "Who exactly would show up? The only people in control in Prague are Alojz and his thugs, and nobody is going to report us to them, not unless they're paid to do so. They don't want to bring that kind of attention on themselves."

"More likely we need to be worried later, when he doesn't return to wherever he came from," J.D. added bending over to finger his charcoal colored clothes. "Men like this rarely work alone. More will come looking for him, but for a short while we're fine. People in this neighborhood tend to keep to themselves."

J.D. turned his gaze back to Abby and looked at her with those eyes that made her feel like he was looking right through her, like he could see and analyze every detail of her appearance and mannerisms. Like she couldn't hide any secrets from him even if she tried. His gaze held hers for a moment longer, long enough that she blushed for some reason. She'd been looked at before, but it had been a while since she'd been really seen by someone who she didn't mind looking at her, like an ex-operative who was not at all bad to look at. Angular face, unshaven, close cropped hair on the sides, with a bit of length on top, and grey eyes. Deep grey eyes.

She shook herself to attention, he'd said something. "What?" she asked, blushing again.

"I said are you alright?"

That sparked some of her fire again. "Of course I am. Why wouldn't I be?"

That took J.D. aback for a moment. He peered at her carefully. "I don't know, I just figured at your age you might not have seen all that many deaths—even on the street."

"I'm not that young," she fired back. "And besides, I saw another one of these men die a few hours ago. I'll be fine."

"What do we do now?" Siggy was pacing nervously around the tiny kitchen-dining area.

"We calm down and think," J.D. responded. Abby couldn't help but admire his coolness under pressure. A dead body in his foyer, a brush with death a moment earlier, and finding out that his strange dinner guest was a Pauser. Most people would have their guts in knots by now. But then, she supposed he was used to this—or at least that he had been, before the PACK dissolved completely, and he went his own way. He was an operative.

"What's there to think about? You said it yourself, he probably works for the warlord, and when he doesn't return it won't be too hard to trace him here. People might not talk voluntarily, but they won't hold anything back if Alojz's thugs come knocking in search of answers. We need to be gone unless we want a real fight on our hands." Siggy was talking rapidly, words piling upon themselves, and Abby had no doubt at all that he was definitely not calm under duress.

"I can uproot pretty quickly," J.D. pondered slowly, as if thinking out loud. "I'll be a little sorry to see the back of this place—Prague was almost starting to feel like home—but I'm not looking to mix it up with Alojz. A surgical assassination strike at him? Sure. But all-out war? No thanks. That's how you get yourself killed."

"And I'm only surprised I stuck around here this long. There's nothing in Prague for me now," Siggy said, a flicker of sadness crossing his face. Abby recognized the all-too-familiar look of one who'd lost their family.

"Well then, it's settled." J.D. grinned at his friend.

Abby felt like an outsider, watching two friends plan the next phase of their lives together. And she supposed that made sense because that was exactly what she was—an outsider.

"In that case, I guess I'd better be going," Abby said, trying to keep the quaver from her voice. "I can take care of myself, and I barely know you. Best of luck."

J.D. stared at her for a long moment before nodding finally. "Luck to you also. Stay to the side streets, find a hideout until dark, and then I suggest you hightail it out of town also."

Abby swallowed back a strange urge to cry. What did she expect? They hardly knew her, and they were only in this mess in the first place because of her. They had no reason to bring her along.

"J.D.!" Siggy hissed.

"What?" the ex-agent said crossly.

"She's too young. We can't just leave her to fend for herself."

"Three's too much trouble," Abby said quickly, "and besides, they're after me—what with my being a special timey-person and all. If you go your own way, you'll be better off." Abby forced as much steel into her voice as possible, hoping against hope that it sounded like strength not bravado. She didn't think she could deal with pity right now.

Pulling the glass knife from her boot, she hefted it. "Plus, it isn't exactly like I'm not armed. I can take care of myself." She didn't sound hollow. She didn't.

"J.D.," Siggy protested again.

J.D. swallowed. "No, she's right. We hardly know her," he began slowly. "Besides, two trails instead of one mean better odds that some of us will escape."

Abby wished he didn't look so guilty as she pursed her lips sadly and walked to the door. She wished it wasn't so strangely painful. For a brief period of time it had almost felt like she had friends again.

"Luck," she said as she opened the door, casting a glance their way before leaving.

"Luck," the ex-agent's voice followed her out the door, into the stairwell, and into the darkness outside.

Abby breathed heavily as she left, keeping an ear trained on the heavens as she'd learned to do, living homeless for so long. Sky-Shatter could happen at any moment. She didn't need them. She would be fine. She could take care of herself. She repeated the litany in her head, over and over again.

She would be fine. She'd survived this long on her own.

She had almost convinced herself it was true, before the scent of sour flesh, and unwashed clothing bombarded her and a hand clasped over her mouth, and a set of powerful arms yanked her screaming into an even darker alley than the street.

# CHAPTER SIX

"It's not right," Siggy was saying hotly.

J.D. winced at his friend's tone.

"Just because she has a pretty pair of eyes and a cute face, doesn't mean we owe her anything," J.D. said.

Siggy gave him a strange look. "What does that have anything to do with it? It's just not right to leave her to fend for herself."

"We'll be safer alone. She's a magnet for trouble in her current state. They're on to her now, and you know as well as I that when people start to manifest special powers like Pausers and Turners do, that they use it more and more frequently until they can gain control of it. And she clearly has no control yet—she's operating entirely on instinct. She'll keep lighting beacons for them, and it'll be best we aren't around when that happens."

Siggy was shaking his head with that disappointed look in his eyes, that look that J.D. hated to see in his friend. J.D. tried to shrug it off. He walked to the balcony and looked out into the night. Off to the side, he could still see the girl's form retreating into the darkness of Prague's narrow, warren of cobblestoned streets.

She would be ok. She had to be.

He swore as he saw a man grab her from the shadows of an alley.

"Stay here," J.D. cried out to his friend and sprang into action. He was out the door and running. Down the stairs, exiting the building into the damp night air. J.D. was sprinting faster than he could remember moving recently, surprising himself with how badly he wanted to reach the girl. Moving quickly enough that his feet were almost slipping on the still-slick cobblestones of Prague, he dashed along the city block toward the alleyway where she'd disappeared.

She had to be ok. He shouldn't have let her leave alone. She was hardly more than a kid, after all.

J.D. reached the entrance to the alley and steeled himself for what he might see as he turned the corner and entered it. All kinds of horrible images flashed through his mind. Abby dead or injured, or perhaps even worse, simply gone, disappeared into the vortex of the warlord's latest greed and desires. She didn't deserve such treatment.

So he was entirely unprepared for what he saw when he did round the corner. Abby was there, not dead, not disappeared, but had her makeshift, street-crafted glass knife in her hand, already covered in blood. The assailant was hunched over and clutching his side. She must have dealt a fairly deep wound to him to make a professional like him stop to regroup.

"Bitch!" the man screamed at her as he straightened up. "I won't go easy on you now. All I have to do is bring you in alive—the rest is up to me."

J.D. could only see the man's back as he was facing away from the alley entrance, but he could practically hear the sneer in the man's voice.

Abby blanched slightly at her attacker's threat. She knew what that meant, knew a man like that was good for it, didn't make threats idly. But she held her knife in front of her with a steady hand. She'd survived years on the street, and J.D. could tell that a girl her age didn't manage that unless she had some true mettle in her. A flash of pride coursed through him, though he barely knew her.

The interaction had only taken a few seconds, from when he'd rounded the corner. He kept his footfalls as silent as possible, moving quickly but quietly toward the back of the man. Abby saw him, and he could see the hope blossom in her eyes, just as the assailant closed in on her again. He was a big man, and even with her weapon, she'd be hard pressed to get out of this situation without help.

J.D. drew his gun even as he slunk up quietly. The man heard him at the last second, but it was too late. Charcoal colored clothes adorned his body as he turned back toward J.D. as if he had an extra sense warning of danger. But it was not quick enough. J.D.'s bullet took the man full in the chest before he could even react. The body hung suspended in midair for a seemingly long millisecond. For half an instant, J.D. wondered if the girl had paused time again as he unloaded two more shots from his clip. But then time warped back to normal, and the shots rang out into the dark night.

The bullet-laden body hit the cobblestones, blood leaking from the wounds in the man's chest and the deep slash in his side. The dark red substance met with the puddles of rainwater and fragments of glass left over in the alley to create an ugly mixture.

"Come on," J.D. reached his hand out to Abby. And then he couldn't resist. "That's twice now." He winked.

"I was fine, you know. I can take care of myself," her words came out flatly, but there was just the faintest hint of uncertainty among them as well as some exasperation.

"Well, you were certainly doing better than I expected, I'll give you that much. We have to go, now."

Abby nodded, and took his symbolically extended hand for just a moment as he led her out of the alley and back onto the street. They dropped hands and slowed their movement to a swift walk, so their behavior wouldn't attract unwanted suspicion.

J.D. noticed that she stowed her glass knife with a swiftness and surety that belied her age, speaking of frequent use. Perhaps even deliberate practice. Yes, she was much tougher than she looked.

"Back to yours?" Abby asked as they walked toward his home.

J.D. nodded. "For a minute or two. Just long enough to collect some personal items, and grab Siggy. I misjudged the situation," he muttered in agitation. "If two were working together then why not a third? Or more? Plus, we've got two dead bodies in the space of a few minutes, and as much as people in this city like to mind their own business, too much ruckus won't go unnoticed. Someone is bound to have notified the warlord's people. It won't be long before we're in serious trouble."

"You don't think tonight's been serious?" Abby's eyebrows shot up incredulously, but to her credit she maintained calm.

Poor kid. She'd had a rough life, but she had no idea what serious was. A few well-placed bullets had ended their difficulties tonight, but there were plenty of situations J.D. could imagine where that wouldn't even be close to the case. They had to move, and quickly.

"Serious enough to make me reconsider Prague," was all he responded.

They took the stairway steps by two as they entered the building, Abby trying to keep up with J.D.'s anxious energy. It wouldn't be long before the enemy showed up in droves.

Funny how an attack on your life and the lives of your friends could instantly frame the world in 'us versus them.' It hadn't been but yesterday that J.D.'s vision of circumstances in Prague had been decidedly nuanced, with opportunity for gain, objectives and more. Now, a few short hours later, events had changed. Two dead thugs spoke of retribution to come. He didn't worry about himself, but Siggy wasn't a violent man, and for all he knew even though Abby handled that knife fairly well, she didn't have the experience that he had to stand up to an army of attackers. No, it was past time to be moving on. J.D. felt a twinge of regret. He might even miss Prague. A little.

He shook off that thought. It would only weaken him. He

should leave this continent behind. How long since he had been back home—true home? Maybe it was time to find a way back across the Atlantic.

They rounded the doorway into his apartment, and J.D. stepped over the dead body of the night's first assailant. Sloppy to leave a door open to a dead body, but he hadn't had a choice. Still, Siggy could have at least tried to take care of it. That irritation increased as Siggy was not in the main kitchen and dining area where J.D. had left him.

"Siggy," he called out.

There was no answer. J.D. did a quick check of the rooms in his apartment, Abby trailing behind silently all the while. No sign of his friend.

"Siggy!" he cried out again, with more urgency and less hope.

He felt a hand on his arm and J.D. looked toward Abby. She was pointing to the table where Siggy's glasses lay, cracked, and battered, but placed there as if very carefully. J.D.'s fears were confirmed by the girl's words.

"I think Siggy's gone."

And then J.D. was astounded at the steel that came out of her mouth next.

"I'll help you get him back—you are planning on getting him back, aren't you?"

# CHAPTER SEVEN

HE STARED AT HER WITH A SURPRISED LOOK IN HIS EYES, AND Abby couldn't for the life of her figure out why that was.

"I said, you *are* going to rescue him, right?"

She saw J.D. visibly shake himself as if clearing his head. "Of course I am. But I'm trained for it—or at least as trained as a person can be. Do you have any idea what you just volunteered to do?"

Abby just shrugged, pretending she didn't feel the fear that was threatening to clamp down on her heart. "I've been in danger before, and I'm sure I will be again."

"Not likely, not like this. Alojz has more men in his compound than you can imagine—courtesy of having a vice grip on the region's resources. You think having a couple people follow you around and try to kidnap you is bad, this will be far worse. And they won't go easy on you anymore if you bring the fight to them."

Abby narrowed her eyes at his warning. "You think he went easy on me in that alley?"

J.D. shook his head. "I think you acquitted yourself well, but I also think he had orders to capture you and bring you in alive and unharmed. If you move against Alojz in force, he'll settle for the former—alive."

"I can take care of myself," Abby said stubbornly, trying to ignore how those words rang false. She'd needed his help just a few minutes ago in the alley, as much as she protested that very fact.

"Are you sure? Really, really sure?" J.D. lowered his voice for added emphasis.

Abby took a deep breath and swallowed. Her instincts were screaming run, but Siggy had wanted to help her, he'd tried to get J.D. to help her. He'd been kind and funny, and one of the first decent human beings she'd spoken with in ages. And he hadn't looked at her with fear when he'd discovered her secret —despite his comments from earlier that night before he'd known. Plus, he was important to J.D., Abby could tell. She wasn't sure why that should matter, but it did.

"I'm sure."

J.D. exhaled slowly. "Well then, we may just have a fighting chance. With my skills and…your abilities, we might be able to get in and get out with all three of us still in one piece." She could see the wheels already turning in his head, planning, strategizing it all out.

"What now?" she asked.

"Now we leave. I'll grab a few things, but then we need to be gone—we should've been gone already."

"And then? Where are we going now?"

J.D. shrugged. "We lay low for a while, plan out the details, and catch our breath. I need time to think, and Siggy won't be any worse off tomorrow than he would be tonight."

"Do you have a place in mind?" Abby prodded.

He shook his head and raised his eyebrows at her as if anticipating her line of thought.

"I know a place," Abby said carefully. "It should be safe for a few hours, at least. I used to go there when I needed a safe place the last few months."

Abby watched J.D. peruse the apartment quickly for items he might need. Most of those items could be found in a bag he'd stashed under the sink. Two more guns, some cash—it was debatable how much good that would do—a change of clothes, a small first aid kit, a canteen full of water, some canned food, and a nasty looking knife. Abby supposed she shouldn't be surprised by his preparedness; it was written into his DNA as a former agent.

In a matter of minutes, they were out the door again and out into the wet night. The rain wasn't falling at the moment, but there was a hint of it still in the air, threatening the skies opening any moment. Abby was just as glad for the lack of noise accompanying the rainless night as she was for the ability to stay dry. Rainy days and nights were more dangerous for travel, since it was harder to hear the deadly shards falling from above when they came.

"You lead," J.D. grunted.

Abby didn't need to be told twice. She'd been on the streets of Prague for months now and knew the warren of alleys and streets as well as she'd known any city in recent memory. She walked swiftly down narrow alleys, turning to muscle-memory. They didn't run—even at night they wanted to be sure to escape attention—but moved at a fast pace, nonetheless. They hugged walls and kept to the shadows. Abby trailed fingertips —exposed to the elements by her fingerless gloves—along the damp stone wall of a building. She regretted it instantly, the chill seeping deeper into her fingers than it seemed to have any right to do. Snow wasn't common in Prague in the winter, but the rain-soaked days and nights of the city could feel almost as chilly.

"A few more streets and we'll be there," she muttered quietly. J.D. didn't answer, but she felt his presence on her hip, close, slightly behind. True to his word he'd followed her, not asking for directions, or trying to take the reins.

His closeness was a comfort. Somehow, after only a few short hours in his presence, he'd managed to win her trust. Her survival instincts screamed that trust was for fools, that she should get away from him, from this place, the first chance she got. But a deeper, older place within her soul felt safe with him. And all of her superficial instincts for keeping herself alive couldn't override that feeling. Besides, he seemed to know as much or more about her...condition, as she did. Perhaps by spending time around him she could gain a better idea of what to expect as her abilities developed.

She led them around a final corner, and they reached their destination. They were on the outskirts of the city center, in an industrial complex—abandoned now. It was a warehouse, the kind that many streetwalkers often used for temporary homes.

But this one was slightly different. For one thing, it looked dilapidated enough that even a desperate urchin would think twice about entering. Beams had fallen, and walls looked on the point of collapse, but Abby knew differently. The collapsing pieces were propped against one another just so, balancing one another and remained intact.

"Doesn't look like much," J.D. muttered as he ducked his head and followed her through a crack in the wall. "You sure it's safe?"

"Oh, it's safe all right."

"How do you know?"

Abby shuddered at the memory but recounted it anyway, the trepidation in his voice inclined her to think that he'd not likely stay in this building if he weren't convinced.

"About a month ago, there was a big storm—"

"—the one that broke so many windows with giant hail balls?" he interjected.

Abby nodded as she led them deeper into the derelict building. "That's the one. Anyway, I was a few blocks away from here when the storm hit and needed a place to crash. I found one of those abandoned stations—I think they were used for trains—anyway lots of us street folk use them. Good enough covering in a pinch, and fairly close to where we want to be. But this time it was only me and one other man taking shelter. He was a mean sort. I could tell by the look on his face."

Abby shivered at the memory. Bearded, unwashed, smelling of old piss and grime, he shouldn't have been anything out of the normal for her kind of people. But it had been his eyes. The devil had been in them. She'd seen it from the moment she crawled in bedraggled and scared, bruised from the few hailstones she hadn't been able to avoid. When his eyes met hers, she'd known right then that all the hail in the world hadn't been more dangerous than that man.

She rushed the story, not eager to relive the moment. "Anyway, he tried to take liberties. I gave him a good kick, in the groin, enough to slow him down. I ran back out into the hailstorm with him on my tail. I lost him quickly but needed a place to lay low—alone this time. That's when I found this old place." She put a hand fondly on the beam she was ducking under as she led him yet further into the middle of the ruin. "After that, I knew I needed protection. I traded for this," she brandished her glass-wrought knife, "and I haven't stopped practicing with it ever since."

"A harrowing story," he said gently, a pain set deep in his eyes. She was glad it wasn't pity. She didn't want his pity. Never that. "But," J.D. continued, "that doesn't exactly explain how you know this place won't collapse on us."

"Oh, right. Well, that storm was in full force, and it blew for hours. I was too scared to leave this place, so I decided to stay put and risk it. It weathered the worst storm I've ever seen without any issues. If it can stand up to the gale force wind and fist-sized hailstones of that night, then I'm pretty certain it'll last for a couple hours more. At least long enough for us to get some rest and keep the shards off our heads."

"Fair enough," J.D. nodded his acceptance.

They settled in and set up 'camp', which consisted of

simply sitting down, J.D. dropping his bag with a weary sound, and slumping against an interior wall that was still intact.

After a few long minutes of silence, Abby broke the stillness. "So, why do you think they took him?"

J.D.'s head was slumped backward against the wall. He cracked open his eyes and rolled his head toward her, still keeping it pressed against the wall. He sighed bitterly. "It could be any number of reasons." He made a disgusted sound and closed his eyes again.

Abby narrowed her eyes. "Are you still drunk?"

He laughed sourly. "No, I suspect the adrenaline burned the majority of the alcohol from my system, much like I'm sure it did for you. In fact, I could probably use a drink. It always steadies my nerves," he mumbled the last bit and clenched his hands into fists.

She'd seen that motion from plenty of riffraff. Street dwellers with the twitches and shakes were a common sight. Had she saddled herself with an alcoholic?

"And those possibilities are?" Abby's voice trailed off, waiting for his response. She spread her hands as he opened his eyes again, waiting for a response.

He sighed again. "Alojz and his men might have grabbed Siggy on purpose—he was looking into some things on my behalf, things regarding the warlord. So it could be my fault. Or," he continued, "it could be revenge. Perhaps I've said no to coming to work for him one too many times. Perhaps he grabbed Siggy as retribution to make me suffer." J.D. shrugged the pain of those thoughts away.

Abby got the distinct impression that he was a man used to

shrugging away many painful things. She understood that emotion more than most people.

"Any other possibilities?"

He nodded in response and held her gaze. "It could simply be opportunistic. And by that, I mean, related to you. You were being chased, they followed you to my place, and when I left to rescue you—don't roll your eyes at me, you may have nicked him in the side but he was about to come at you full force—"

"—nicked him?" Abby muttered in annoyance. "Did you see how much blood he was losing?"

"Yes, I did, all the more reason he had to pay you back in kind. Anyway, it's possible the others in support of those two—the one who attacked us and the one who grabbed you outside—saw me leave and went to check on their compatriot. Seeing he was dead, and Siggy was alone, they simply grabbed him because they could."

"So, it's my fault he was taken." She tried to keep her voice from sounding so small. She swallowed.

"Hey, look at me."

Abby turned her head as if compelled somehow. She stared at J.D.'s surprisingly compassionate face. His eyes were a deep grey.

"I didn't say it was your fault. It's not. It's that asshole Alojz's fault."

Abby nodded, not trusting herself to speak. Siggy had possessed an innocence about him, the kind she no longer had after her time on the streets, the kind J.D. might never have had. She looked at the ex-agent next to her. He had to have been a child at some point, but all she could see was a bitterly sarcastic exterior, that concealed pain, and a set of skills that were dangerous at best and horrific at worst. Yet there was a depth to J.D. that she found surprising. Perhaps it was the age difference between them. He'd seen a lot more of the world than she. More than this god-forsaken stretch of land in New Central Europe.

Abby found herself suddenly missing home, a home she hadn't seen in many years, since before her parents moved her into this region when they'd accepted the positions with PACK. She missed the faint mist of the Federation of the Isles, constant, but not loud like the rain here. The quiet damp of the isles didn't carry with it the danger of rain elsewhere, didn't mask the falling danger from above except on rare occasions. At least, not where she'd grown up.

"What?" J.D. asked her, a strange look in his eye.

"Nothing, just thinking of home for a second." She blushed. He must think her a child.

But all he did was nod. He was far from home too, she realized. Farther than her, and he'd likely been gone longer.

She didn't particularly like vulnerability. It was time to change the subject. "So, what's the plan? How do we go about rescuing dear old Sigmund?"

# CHAPTER EIGHT

J.D. LOOKED AT THE GIRL BESIDE HIM. ABBY WAS PUTTING ON a brave face. She was certainly tougher than he'd been at that age. At nineteen, he'd been hardly more than an overgrown child. It had taken him years of training to cope with disaster and danger the way she was already able to do. But she was scared. He could see the fear simmering below a thin veneer of nonchalance and jokes, behind a mask of stoic toughness that had likely gotten her through some difficult times alone on the streets.

City-States didn't have the same rule of law and citizen's rights that the ancient nations had strived to possess. And even when they did, those laws tended to be heavily skewed in favor of those whom the feudal-esque lord felt like favoring. It certainly didn't apply to those who were disenfranchised and at the edges of an already fraying society.

"You're sure you want to do this? Even with your help, at absolute best, I'd give us less than fifty-fifty odds of success—

and by success, you do know I mean survival." J.D. peered at her carefully, weighing up her response. He couldn't take someone with him into danger if they weren't committed to seeing it through.

She shrugged casually. "You act like I've never been in danger before. Have you forgotten the past 12 hours or the story I just told you a few minutes ago?"

J.D. admired her resolve—her determination to appear determined. He could still see the anxiety bubbling, just like it was in the pit of his belly as well. He just hid it better, had more years of practice. He decided to honor her word. A simple nod and he moved on.

"We'll need to move quickly and silently when the time comes. In the past, out of curiosity, I've scouted around the fortress on the hill where Alojz keeps his makeshift court. It's a solidly defensible position against an army, but it has a few cracks. With just two of us, we should be able to make it in unnoticed."

"And then?"

He tilted his head in a half shrug. "We don't have time to waste in reconnaissance. Alojz isn't known for being overly patient. Whatever he has planned for Siggy won't happen tonight, but it will happen sooner rather than later. We'll head for the most likely location and get him out."

"That is brilliantly basic, you know. Is that what they trained you to do as a Wolf? No wonder PACK fell apart." She rolled her eyes with a laugh.

J.D. winked. "Storm the castle and all that."

She shook her head. J.D. appreciated that she was smart

enough to understand the difficulty of the situation. "What do we have around here for a last meal?" she inquired.

J.D. pulled a can of beans from his pack. "My fifty-fifty odds might have been generous. If they don't kill us, these certainly will." He pried open the lid with his heavy combat knife, serrated on one edge, being careful to avoid the newly jagged rim of the can.

Abby wrinkled her nose.

"Cold beans not good enough for you?" he teased. "I'd have thought you would have a stronger stomach living like you have these last years."

"I eat what I have to for survival. That doesn't mean I have to like it." Still she reached her hand over and dug her fingers into the mess of beans.

"Careful not to cut yourself," he warned.

She flashed him an annoyed look. "I'm not an idiot."

He laughed. "Alright, I know that. Relax."

They traded bites for a while. And then the silence stretched again. Strangely enough, it was a comfortable silence —at least for him it was. It felt like they'd known each other a lot longer than a few hours. He might have been surprised by the notion, but he'd been through adrenaline packed days before. J.D. knew how quickly shared danger and sacrifice could bond people together. Just the fact that she was willing to go into her pursuers' stronghold to help him get back someone she barely knew was enough to win him over. The girl had guts and heart, no denying it.

"Seriously, though. What's the plan? You were decidedly vague earlier," she said.

J.D. sighed. He'd been doing that a lot tonight. "I don't honestly have much more of a plan." He hefted his gun and then jiggled the bag to his left to indicate his other weaponry. "I'm trained to use these and use them I will. I'm a match for any of them one on one, and with a few extra clips and the darkness to hide me, I should be able to take out a lot of them. Get one alone early, maybe even do a quick interrogation to confirm what I suspect." He grimaced at having to mention that in front of Abby. She was still young enough that he didn't want her dwelling on how messy it could get. But she didn't flinch, didn't even react when he said it. She was tough, all right.

"So where do I come in?"

"You... well you stay close to me, but out of the way."

"And?"

"And if you can tap into your magic thingy," he wiggled his fingers mysteriously and made a face, "then so much the better."

"That's it?" She muttered at his response again.

"Do you have a better idea? From what you said earlier, you've only ever Paused a couple of times. You aren't trained and don't know how to do it on command. The best we can hope for is that your adrenaline spikes and you do it instinctively. Maybe if we had a few months for you to practice and get stronger... but we don't."

Abby made a frustrated sound but didn't disagree. She knew he was right. Instead she changed her line of questioning again. "So, you said we wait for dark?"

J.D. nodded. "We don't want to go tonight. We need rest to

be sharp, since Siggy can't afford us operating at anything less. That means tomorrow night. We don't want to wait any longer than that."

Her mouth twisted up in a nervous grimace. "Waiting all day isn't going to be easy."

"Try to sleep. Try not to think. Just take the rest while you can get it. God knows we likely won't get the chance again for a while, even if all goes perfectly. We'll still have to leave Prague in a hurry, likely with pursuit hot on our trail."

"How are we going to leave?" Abby stifled a yawn and leaned her head back against the wall like J.D. was already doing.

"You ask too many questions," J.D. shot back, with a half-smile on his face. "Damn, I could really use a drink right now. Whiskey would be sublime."

"Drunkard."

His eyes were closed as he felt her slide her head onto his shoulder. He heard her measured breaths, a calming influence as he struggled to quiet his mind and find some sleep.

J.D. hoped for a dreamless sleep, and he was rewarded.

———

Abby woke from a clammy doze with J.D.'s hand on her shoulder. They'd been resting and sleeping, storing as much energy as they could over the course of the day.

"It's nearly twilight. Time we were heading toward the castle on the hill. We want to be in position when nightfall arrives." J.D. squatted next to her and spoke quietly, hardly more than a whisper, even though there was no need in such a secluded, ramshackle structure. Nobody was nearby to hear. But Abby understood. She nodded silently and stood, already embracing the silence they would need in order to be successful tonight.

They ate a few last bites from the bag of supplies J.D. had hurriedly gathered before leaving last night, then left the abandoned building. Abby took the lead, winding through fallen beams and leaning walls. This hidey hole, this derelict structure, this was her domain. Street walker, Time Fighter, Pauser. Runner. She'd likely be running her whole life.

As soon as they were free from the ruins, she let J.D. lead the way as they made their way through the city. Prague was relatively quiet, but they still stuck to side streets. At a break in the buildings, Abby saw the sharp, steepled roofs of twin towers near the city center, but they stayed well away from that area. Red roofs and colorful facades passed as they made their way to the Charles Bridge and then across. Not an overly long bridge, but wide open. After all her time on the streets, being out in the open like this made the space between her shoulders itch. Abby was glad to be across and back among buildings again as they stepped foot off the causeway.

J.D. pulled her by the hand into the shadows of an alley. "It's time to slow down and start being more careful," he murmured, his mouth practically in her ear, speaking so quietly only she could hear.

"Haven't we already been doing that?" she retorted. Their pace had been hardly more than a crawl at times.

J.D. rolled his eyes as if they'd known each other longer

than just a day. "Enough. Seriously, from here on out, I need to know you'll do what I say, without question."

"But questioning is what I'm good at!" she pouted, hoping he could see the twinkle that must be in her eyes. She knew she shouldn't be joking around right now, but the danger they were heading into was making her strangely giddy. Was that normal? She opened her mouth to ask J.D., but he flippantly pinched her lips together with his thumb and first two fingers.

"What did I just say?" he breathed in annoyance. This time it was Abby's turn to roll her eyes. She shrugged non-committedly and motioned for him to continue.

J.D. spoke when he was certain she was quiet and listening. "From here we stick to the alleys and shadows. I've scouted around here in the past—it always pays to know your neighbors, and it turns out I was right—so I know there's an entrance to the fortress on the far side from here. Lightly guarded as well. This hilltop castle might be imposing, but its old. It's hardly impregnable. We'll slip through the cracks undetected." He shrugged reluctantly. "And if we can't, then we dispose of any threats we can't avoid as quietly as possible."

Abby nodded in agreement, still obeying his call for silence. He smiled in approval, and she felt a flash of annoyance at the fact that she was happy for the approval.

"One more thing," J.D. whispered, "I know you've come along because of what you can do. But I've seen Pausers in their prime, in full use of their powers." She saw him swallow involuntarily, as if it were enough to make even a hardened ex-agent like him nervous, "and as dangerous as they are, they aren't invulnerable. And you're nowhere near trained or in control of your abilities."

He lifted a hand to forestall the reactionary argument that was already bubbling on her lips. "Stop, we both know it's true. A handful of Pauses does not a Time Fighter make. We don't even know if there's a limit to what you can do or how often. So don't waste it. I can handle small numbers of assailants. I'll need your help if we come across anything where the odds are significantly against me, but for the most part, I'm trained to deal with most small numbers of attackers. Okay?"

He gazed into her eyes. This close his were deep pools, mysterious and hard, but strangely comforting. She nodded again silently.

Finally, she spoke. "I follow you. I do what you say. I stay quiet. I only try and access my abilities and use them in a last-ditch emergency." She cocked her head and stared back at him. "Sufficient to impress upon you that I have the memory of a five-year-old?"

This time he chuckled. "Fine. I trust you. But don't forget what you just repeated back to me in the heat of the moment. Ready?"

"One last question."

J.D. fixed her a look, but waited impatiently, nonetheless.

Abby swallowed. "Assuming we can get to Siggy and get him out, are you also going to take advantage of where we are and try to get ahold of the intel Siggy's been trying to get for you?"

J.D. sighed. "We all have to move on sometime."

Abby raised her eyebrows at him in question.

"I've been holding on to an old mission. Old objectives, hoping, wishing for a return to where we used to be." He waved his hand vaguely as if indicating society as a whole. "It doesn't serve anybody to dwell in the past. We all have to move on." He shot a pointed look her way, and she flushed slightly, even though she wasn't sure exactly what he meant by it.

"So, mission accomplished?" she queried.

"More like mission aborted," he snorted. "But Siggy safe and us on the run is better than getting intel on a dead mission. It was a waste of time anyway."

Abby nodded, finally done asking questions. "Ready."

J.D. grinned and winked despite the gravity of what they were about to attempt, then he turned and led her further into the dark, trusting that she would follow.

She did.

# CHAPTER NINE

J.D. HAD TO KILL ONE MERCENARY BEFORE THEY EVEN reached the outer wall of the fortress. A thick, broad-shouldered man with a grey-tinged beard saw them slinking in the shadows making their way ever nearer to the wall. As J.D. heard the skitter of small pebbles as the patrol rounded the corner, their eyes had met, and J.D. had seen the shrewd look of an aging professional, a soldier who'd been through the wars literally and figuratively. There was no playing off their proximity to the castle.

J.D. had reacted instantaneously, instinctually. Luckily, his knife had already been drawn and ready as they prowled closer to the fortress. Before the other man could blink, he released the knife with a steady—albeit slightly rushed—cast of the weapon, sending it spinning towards his enemy. The man opened his mouth to shout an alarm, but the weapon struck home too quickly. It wasn't a killing toss, but a knife in the stomach had a way of shutting a man up, sucking the wind right from his lungs. J.D. was on him in a flash, wrenching the knife out and slitting the man's throat. J.D. saw the flashes of startled anger in his eyes as the light in them faded out.

"Why did you stare at him like that? Shouldn't we be moving on?" Abby asked.

J.D. turned toward her voice, her body still hugging the shadows against a wall. She wouldn't need to do so much longer. Full night was basically upon them.

Shrugging almost self-consciously, he replied, "He didn't get to raise the alarm, so we have more time than you think. Kill enough people and you'll realize that if you can honor their last moment, look them in the eye as they go, then you owe them that. If you can."

"Have you killed that many?" the girl asked quietly.

He shook his head. "Are we here to help a friend or for a history lesson?" he muttered irritably as he dragged the man into the alley jutting off the street, pocketing the man's keys as he did so. Perhaps they'd be useful later. Hopefully, that would be sufficient to conceal the dead man until they accomplished their goals for the night. But J.D. didn't expect it would be. Things never quite went according to plan on ventures like these. If they did, then there would've been a whole lot more people like him alive and active.

They moved on quietly, quickly making their way along the narrow streets approaching the fortress. They saw one or two more guards along the way, but always with enough time to conceal themselves and avoid detection. Before long they turned another corner, and he put a hand on Abby's shoulder to bring her to a halt.

"Do you see that gateway?" He pointed to the door in the wall, maybe forty yards away. She nodded tersely. She was holding up well, all things considered, but it was clear to J.D. that her nerves were on a razor's edge.

"Wait for me here. I'll go open it from the inside and let you in."

"How?" she whispered.

"There's a lower, rougher stretch of wall just over there," he pointed vaguely off into the near distance. "I targeted it as a weak point the last time I was doing some reconnaissance around here. I'll climb it, and then circle back to quietly take care of the guards at the gate, letting you in."

"Why can't I just climb also?"

J.D. looked at her, quirking an eyebrow. "Do you have a head for heights—do you even know if you do? Not a good idea to get fifty feet up on a wall with only modest handholds still slightly damp from today's rain and not know for certain. Accidents at that height are usually fatal." He paused, looking at her.

She kept her mouth shut in a thin nervous line.

"No?" he continued. "Well then, I think we'll stick to my plan, alright?" She nodded her agreement, however reluctantly.

"How long will it take?" she asked, brushing some hair out of her face.

"If I haven't opened the gate for you in fifteen minutes, then I'm not going to. In that case you run. You get out of here —out of the city. You cover as much ground as you can, get as far away from here as possible, and you never look back. Got it?"

Abby swallowed and then nodded again.

"They already know about you, what you can do. If you stay anywhere within Alojz's reach, he'll never stop hunting you." J.D. paused noticing the fear on her face. His tone softened. "Don't worry. A quick climb and a few guards are nothing I can't handle. That gate will be open in no time at all."

Abby smiled at him, looking somewhat relieved but still worried. "If you say so. You seem a bit out of shape and out of practice to me."

J.D. snorted. He cuffed her chin good-naturedly. "Wait for me. There's enough light by the gate that you'll have no trouble seeing my signal for when it's safe to follow." With that he turned and sprinted lithely along the wall, hugging the darkness outside of the lamplight. Before more than a minute had passed, he'd run around a bend and out of sight of her.

J.D. huffed slightly as he approached the wall. The girl wasn't wrong. He *was* out of shape. He set his hands to the rough spaces in the wall, the gaps he'd noticed last time he was here, and started to climb. Patrols were frequent up along the parapet. He'd need some luck to avoid reaching the top just as one of them passed. But it wouldn't be a true covert mission without a little risk. He'd lived for it back before the PACK had collapsed, and sure enough, he found the adrenaline that spiked in his body thrilling.

About two-thirds of the way up the climb—five minutes in —a faint tinkling sounded from above. *Guards and their keys?* he wondered curiously. But the guard he'd killed hadn't sounded like that as he'd moved, regardless of the small set of keys he'd possessed. The tinkling continued uninterrupted and

J.D. swore softly as realization hit him. He pressed himself tightly to the wall, spreading his body against it, compromising his grasp ever so slightly. He had to though—there was no other choice. In an exposed situation like this, a shard of glass would kill him, and if it didn't, the fall it caused certainly would.

Sure enough, a rain of shards fell around him. Some struck the parapet and wall above him, while others fell to the ground below. A few nicked his arms as they went by, big enough to slice through his sleeves. But nothing bad enough to send him careening into the dark below. As his grip was just slipping, the sound stopped, signaling it was time to continue. He quickly pulled himself the rest of the way up the wall, eager to get out from the compromised position. He hauled himself over the lip just as a guard rounded the bend. Just his luck. But surprisingly, fortune was shining on J.D. because the guard stumbled slightly, clearly drunk, not possessing the keen eyes of the dead man in the alley. The mercenary stumbled closer to J.D., who was crouched by the wall, shadows ensconcing him.

Closer. Closer.

When the man was only a few feet away J.D. leaped at him. A surprised gurgle left the man's throat but nothing more, since J.D.'s arm was around it and choking him as he swung himself behind the guard. A simple flex of his muscles and the vice tightened, cutting off air and rendering the man unconscious. J.D. laid him quietly on the walkway, the slight crunch of leftover, shattered glass underfoot and under the man's body. J.D. thought for a moment about leaving him unconscious, but there was no consistency to when he might wake up. It could be seconds or minutes. Either way, he would raise the alarm. Almost regretfully, J.D. slid his knife along the man's throat and then turned to make his way back toward the gate and the girl waiting.

———

Abby waited impatiently, worriedly, in the dark. Lamplight from above the gate shone down, making this section of the wall and the area around it lighter than many of the other's they'd passed. It made her uncomfortable.

She didn't possess a watch, so she counted. Old fashioned perhaps, but better than estimation. J.D. had said fifteen minutes. She didn't think he'd have exaggerated. If he weren't signaling her by then, Abby was going to turn tail and run as fast and as carefully as she could. She might have just met him, but she trusted him enough on this. Trusted her instincts as well. Although truth be told, those instincts were already screaming at her—had been screaming at her for hours now—to get out of here, to run. What was she doing, trying to help rescue someone she'd only met yesterday? Was she that desperate for companionship? A deep, lonely part of her shied away from that question. No, she was keeping her word, that's what she was doing. She'd said she would help, so she was.

Four minutes. Had it really only been that long?

Nine minutes.

Twelve minutes. Maybe he had run into trouble. Maybe she should run already. He wouldn't want her to go down with him; they might have just met, but she knew enough about him to know he didn't want her to get hurt. She saw the strange protectiveness in his eyes at times when he didn't think she would notice.

Fourteen minutes. Her counting was reaching a fever pitch in her mind. Frantic, even in the silence.

Fifteen.

And the gate swung open—cracked open more like—and a hand beckoned. She glanced around, and then sprinted, deer-like, toward the opening.

Abby ducked through as the gate fastened closed behind her, and the first things she saw were the two dead men.

"It was quick and quiet, nobody heard," J.D. grunted. "One more on the wall above, but it was the same. We should still be safe. For now. Too many more go missing, and they'll start to notice. We need to move fast now."

He grasped her hand and pulled Abby after him. Not for the first time she wondered how she'd gotten caught up with a man who was a whirlwind of death. But strangely, it didn't spark fear in her. Instead, it created an odd comfort, a feeling of safety that with him around she would be alright. Somewhere in the recesses of her mind, she knew it wasn't true, that anyone could die, *would* die. But around J.D., it felt like they might survive anything.

The fortress inside the wall was a mix-match of building styles as if it had been gradually erected and renovated throughout many years. Some structures looked like they were a half-millennia old, others less, and some newer buildings amongst them even looked almost modern, like they had been built in the twenty-first century before the troubles of the last age.

J.D. moved ahead of her, slinking between outcroppings and walls, clinging to the shadows, as was necessary with more lamplight to illuminate their surroundings than there had been outside. Alojz might feel secure and safe in his castle, with his thugs around him and no real powers within close striking distance, but he wasn't taking chances. Patrols were everywhere, and Abby was hard-pressed to keep up with the ex-agent leading her. J.D. was a shadowy blur before her, dodging patrols, as if he had foresight for where they'd be. Stopping her when necessary and then moving again. It was like he was part of some current, tied to his surroundings, able to sense and feel the right time to move and go, stop and stay. Abby would have wondered if he had powers of his own— something akin to her abilities as a Pauser—were it not for the fact that she knew his past. She realized he'd probably spent years of his life training for and then executing excursions such as this. Even a few years removed, he wouldn't have forgotten. It would be muscle memory, instinct.

As J.D. pulled her close to him, pressed against a wall, close enough to feel the heat emanating off his body in the chill night, she chanced a question. "Where are we going? Do you know where Siggy is being kept?"

J.D. cut her an annoyed look but answered anyway. "I told you I did some reconnaissance of these grounds not long after I arrived in Prague a couple years back. As soon as it became clear that my presence had become known to Alojz, I couldn't afford to be ill-informed." He broke off and went silent as a patrol walked toward the wall a few dozen yards away. Likely replacements. Abby thought nervously of the dead men her partner in crime had left behind. It wouldn't be long before their presence would be detected. She waited for J.D. to finish his thought as the men slowly disappeared, in no rush to get to their post. Mercenaries were hardly the most reliable or committed men. And yet most warlords relied upon them almost exclusively, with little allegiance to be found elsewhere. It was a vicious circle—without allegiance they hired mercenaries, who required higher pay, meaning resources had to be squeezed from the surrounding land, engendering little goodwill and even less allegiance going forward. An iron fist was required in the City-States. At least, that was how Abby remembered her parents describing things to her. Prague certainly seemed to be no different.

"And…?" she prodded J.D. when it became clear he wasn't inclined to finish.

He sighed. "I didn't have a chance to question anybody tonight—it just didn't work out that way this time—but a part of my prior reconnaissance was ambushing one of his thugs in town and extracting information."

"He told you ahead of time where Siggy would be kept?" Abby's forehead creased.

J.D. shot her a look that made her feel foolish. "No. But I picked his brain for any and all information about this compound—weak points, manpower, Alojz's quarters, and of course, prisoner housing facilities."

Realization dawned on Abby and she felt silly for not having understood. Adrenaline must be clouding her head.

"You're leading us to the jail." J.D. inclined his head, but she continued, "But what if he's being held elsewhere?"

Her friend assumed a grim mask. "It's most likely he's in the jail. And if he's not, but rather in some random room in an arbitrary building, then we were never likely to find him in the first place, and this whole thing was doomed to fail."

She cocked her head at him.

"Look," he sighed, "the alarm is going to go up any time now, and if we were to try to slowly, quietly search every room in this place for Siggy, we'd need all the luck in the world to find him in time. Our best—no, our only—chance was and still is to head straight for the prisoner holdings, hope he's there, and then bust him out."

"And if he's not? There, I mean."

If it were possible J.D.'s face became grimmer. "Then we abandon ship and try and get out of here with our hides still intact."

"Just leave him?" For some reason, Abby couldn't believe that she'd just heard what she thought she had. "He's your best friend!"

"Did I ever say that?" J.D. huffed, then relented. "Well, he probably is at that, if I felt like describing him with a grade school adjective. But that doesn't change anything. You're right, we are friends, good enough friends that Siggy would never want me—or you—to die for him. Not in vain. And believe me, this place is big enough that a random search would be in vain."

Abby swallowed, pondering it all. But she wasn't given any

more time to think or talk, because J.D.'s hand was on hers, pulling her forward.

As he led her in a crouching run across a courtyard, he whispered, "That building ahead of us is the jail." He indicated a building with a brightly colored façade, not at all what she would have pictured as a prison building. It was straight out of the 17th century, and still a few dozen yards away.

This building had guards, and there was no way to sneak by them. A muffled shout in the night went up as the two men posted outside the door saw the two of them approaching.

J.D. swore, although Abby didn't think he'd expected anything other than this; there was simply too much open space between them and the guards.

"Here we go," J.D. muttered. "Remember, stay behind me and out of the way if you can. And try not to waste your power on odds as good as this!" And with that, the ex-agent pulled two handguns out from where they had been hidden beneath his coat and fired as he ran.

The loudness of the gunshots in what had been a previously silent night were a shock to Abby's system, and her adrenaline spiked even as the two men guarding the door fell, one with a bullet to the chest, never to rise again, the other as one of J.D.'s bullets sprayed his shoulder. The man struggled back to his feet as they closed the distance, getting off a shot of his own with a pistol. Abby clutched her crude, glass knife tightly—when had she pulled it?—and watched as J.D. tucked one of his guns away, tackled the man, and stuck his own knife into the man's gut and twisted.

The death was quick but messy. The man screamed, but it

didn't really matter, because by that point the alarm had already been raised. Abby could hear the shouts of surprise and chaos as men rushed to find the source of the alarm. J.D. scooped the keys out of the man's pocket, but didn't bother to find the proper key, he just kicked through the door in his rush. Abby followed him through it, trying not to vomit as she saw the dead man's innards spread across the cobblestones of the courtyard.

Inside, they found a darkened building, old, matching the façade, but it was still a fairly simple matter to find the cells. This particular structure seemed to only be used as a jail, so they only had to bypass a couple cells before they found the one they were looking for. Luck was with them.

Siggy lay in a pile on the ground, unconscious it seemed. They had roughed him up badly. His face was a messy pulp, one eye puffy. Cuts along his face and hands had leaked blood all over him. *Did they go after him with knives?* Abby couldn't help but wonder with a sick fascination.

J.D. rushed to the cell door, swearing and fumbling for the right key. "Shit, Siggy, what did they do to you? Wake up buddy. Wake up, Sigmund, damn it!" By the end, as he finally found the right key and unlocked the barred door, Siggy was finally stirring.

"Wh-what? Is that you J.D.?" the young man asked blearily, straining to see in the dark and through his puffed-up eye.

"It's me, Siggy, it's me—and Abby," he added. "Come on, we gotta go." He tried to help Siggy to his feet, but the young man could barely stand, and in the end, J.D. just slung him over his shoulder and half-carried, half-dragged him out of the cell and toward the jail entrance. Abby wormed her way under Siggy's other arm, wishing she knew what to do and how to be of more help. She was beginning to feel next to useless. What had she even done to help J.D. tonight? He'd have been faster, safer, better off without her along. Bitterness flooded in. What had she been thinking? Everyone would be safer without her around. Without her, Siggy likely wouldn't even be in this situation. Abby followed them into the night air.

"Come on, Siggy, you have to stand, you have to walk. I can't carry you the whole way."

Gunshots sounded and bullets ricocheted off the wall near them. J.D. pulled one gun and fired a few back towards the men who were closing in on them. Siggy finally found his feet, although he seemed to be moving groggily still. Abby stepped up quickly and put an arm under his shoulder to a mumbled thanks.

J.D. pulled both guns now and was firing with both hands. Men were sprinting toward them, taking cover as his bullets flew near them. One dropped as J.D.'s bullet hit home.

"Where are we going?" Abby screamed amidst the chaos of shouts and gunfire. They were awfully exposed standing against the wall. "Back to the gate?"

J.D. turned a harried almost fearful face her way. "No time. It's too far from here and there are too many of them."

"What! What's the plan then?"

He shook his head. "A crazy one, I think. Follow me."

He motioned for them to follow, and they stumbled after him, as he lay down cover fire to keep the mercenaries at bay.

It wouldn't last forever. Already they were getting closer; there were too many of them to keep them all back, regardless of how deadly J.D. was with his pistols. The soldiers herded them away from the gate where they'd entered.

J.D. led them uphill slightly, toward a cleared patch in the middle of the fortress, a square of sorts. Abby saw what they were aiming for. A helicopter stood in the middle of the grounds and as of that moment it was still undefended, with most of the men following behind them.

"You know how to fly one of those?" Abby shouted shakily over the noise. Her parents had spoken of choppers as if they were very dangerous. As society devolved, training had decreased for flying contraptions like that, until deaths became more and more common. Fuel had also become scarce, causing flights to only happen occasionally, again leading to less skillful and experienced pilots. In all, it sounded like disaster happened as often as not when they'd been employed over the past half century.

J.D. shot her a fevered grin. "I may have learned a thing or two in my training. Read some pilot theory."

"But you've never actually flown?" She gaped incredulously.

He shrugged in desperation. "Does a simulator count?"

She wanted to scream no, of course a simulator didn't count! But in truth she didn't see as they had much choice.

He grimaced. "Look, I knew it was here from when I scouted in the past, but it was never my plan A for escape. Events force your hand sometime," he finished grimly.

Abby stumbled onward, calling on all her strength to keep

Siggy upright as J.D. fired shot after shot, feeding extra clips into his gun from somewhere they'd been stashed on his body. They drew closer and closer to the helicopter, until Abby began to think that just maybe they had a chance.

Until from another side of the open square men burst out of a building and came toward them at a dead sprint.

"J.D.!" She cried the warning since the men were behind him. He turned just in time to get off one shot in their direction before Abby saw him spin horribly, lifelessly to the ground as a bullet found its mark.

# CHAPTER TEN

J.D. LAY ON THE GROUND STUNNED. PAIN RIPPED THROUGH HIS shoulder, radiating outward. He groaned, but the sound felt far away, as it was hard to hear himself through the fog of agony. He struggled to prop himself up. He shook his head to clear it, fighting to not wilt back to the ground beneath the pain of the gunshot wound.

"Abby, Siggy," he mumbled blearily to himself. His eyes searched and found them a few yards away, almost to the chopper. He fought to regain his feet as men converged on them. He fired off a few shots that didn't come close to anyone.

"J.D.!" Abby was still shouting. "Hurry!"

He fired off more shots, his aim improving again as he winged one man and put another down. He could barely lift his injured arm for the pain, but he gritted his teeth and did anyway. You quit when you died.

Gunshots came in a flurry as he backed toward the chopper, but they'd never get it going before the men caught them. He killed another with a well-aimed bullet, and then they were upon him.

Even with an injured shoulder, he was more than a match for any one of them. They were mercenaries, thugs who'd been hired to play soldier and beat up locals, enforce the warlord's will on the region. They weren't trained like him, weren't a Wolf like him.

But there were so many of them. Too many.

As they closed in, he holstered his guns and drew knives—one his PACK-grade metal combat knife with a serrated edge, the other a homemade street knife made of shard and cloth. Slashing and fighting through the tearing pain of his gunshot wound, he slit throats and gutted men. He even ducked low and hamstrung one of the thugs, who fell to the ground with a strangled shriek. But he took wounds himself—slashes here, a deep gash along his right ribs, opposite his shoulder injury—and they slowed him down further.

He turned from wrenching his knife out of the belly of an assailant to find a club descending toward his face, only for the man to crumple at the last moment. J.D. turned, stunned to see Siggy holding a gun in a wobbly hand. He must have picked it up from a dead mercenary. J.D. chanced a glance at the girl. Her eyes were shut. Was it pure terror? Some people folded completely in life-threatening situations. He'd seen it time and again during his training and then in the field. He never should have brought her with him. She would die here or be captured and become a plaything for Alojz.

He wasn't sure which was the worse fate. He'd heard all sorts of rumors about the warlord. Oh, he knew Abby's secret, he wouldn't kill the girl, but Alojz would see anything else as free game.

She squeezed her eyes more tightly together if that were possible, it almost looked like she was murmuring a prayer. Then it dawned on him. She wasn't wilting or crying. She wasn't going comatose.

She was *trying*. Trying to Pause time.

Now it was J.D.'s turn to pray. If she could do it, then they might even have a chance. But nothing happened, and he turned back to the fray, swinging his leaden arms, shattering knees with kicks as best he could. He heard gunfire again and hoped it was Siggy dispatching another mercenary and not the other way around. He fought until he was forced back almost to the chopper when he heard it. Over the noise and ruckus, he heard the clinking shriek of falling glass.

"Abby!" He turned to shout at her, but she had clearly heard it also as she opened her eyes and her gaze found his. "Get under the helicopter," he mouthed, not wishing to alert their enemies. Siggy was bright and had already figured it out, but he was closer than J.D. to the machine, and could make it in time. J.D. couldn't. And he knew it.

He swung a knife at another man, determined to go down swinging, slashing a throat before ducking his head and covering it with his hands, hoping, praying that he'd survive the falling shards.

Glass careened downward shrieking even as it clattered together like a horrific wind chime. Pieces skewered men left and right. One sliced through his injured arm, causing a red line of pain to streak across his brain. Cries of the wounded and dying pierced the night, then silence punctuated by groans.

J.D. lifted his hand from his head and got up from his crouch. Somehow, he was still alive. He shouldn't have survived a rain of glass like that in the open. He should be dead like most of the men around him. He looked worriedly back toward the chopper and was relieved to see that Siggy and Abby were underneath, kept safe by the hunk of metal above them.

A few men struggled to their feet, injured like he was. But worse were the shouts and cries of more men making their way to the square. Were there really more men in the warlord's service? J.D. almost groaned out loud as they rounded into sight from one of the compound's nearby alleys only a few dozen yards away. They closed the distance faster than he would have imagined. Losing blood and exhausted, one arm hanging limply, he didn't even know if he could make it the few feet to the helicopter before they reached him. So close to escape, and yet too far away. He turned to face the men as a piercing scream of fear echoed through the courtyard behind him.

———

Abby saw more men coming into view, saw J.D. turn to hopelessly confront them. It wasn't fair! They were so close to escape. When she felt the knife at her throat and hot breath steaming in her ear, she nearly wilted in fear.

"I've been looking for you, bitch, and here you went

through all the trouble to come to me. I just didn't think it would cost me half my men to get you. You'll pay for bringing the Wolf down upon me!" Alojz snarled. The knife bit into her skin, just enough to send a trickle of warmth dripping slowly down her neck.

"Just take me, let them go," she pleaded.

"Too late for that, sweetheart," Alojz gloated. "I'll kill them slowly for what they've cost me."

"No!" The cry came to her lips unbidden, even as that unknown switch within her flipped and time stopped. It had *happened* again. For all her trying during the fight she'd had no success. Until now.

Abby wriggled free of his sweaty grasp as the warlord of the City-State of Prague stood frozen in the night. She pulled her glass knife and thought about what J.D. would do.

There was no telling how long this Pause would last, her mind calculated hurriedly. It had never lasted overly long and could last only seconds. She had to think fast. The world stood still around her, friend and foe alike. Siggy had his head turned her way, glassy eyes staring vacantly into the void of nothing-time, the in between, in which she now stood and operated.

J.D. would kill Alojz. Of that she was certain. Only she wasn't sure she could, didn't know if she was that hardened from her time on the streets. Hard enough to survive, but to murder in cold blood a man—albeit an ugly-souled man—who was defenseless against her?

In the end she gripped her cloth-wrapped knife handle and opted to plunge the glass knife into his guts and twist. His skin parted and gave, and she knew she'd delivered a wound that was too deep to ignore, that would buy her time when the world restarted, but in this frozen moment the warlord didn't make a sound, didn't even register the pain of the wound as his eyes looked beyond her. The silent injury was eerily more terrifying than the fact that she had just delivered a grievous wound to an unprotected man.

No more time for thought. She ran to the ex-agent who was looking back over his shoulder toward her initial position at the helicopter. The moment wouldn't last much longer. Abby, strained with her will, her mind, to keep the freeze intact. She grabbed J.D.'s arm and tried to tug him with her, but his body strangely resisted the motion.

There had to be a solution. She could leave. The thought came unbidden and filled her with shame. Could she though? From their discussion earlier, the Wolf would likely applaud her decision, be relieved she'd gotten away safely, even if it meant leaving them behind. He'd said as much of Siggy. But could she do it? Was that who the real Abigail was, deep down in the core of her being?

No.

No, she wouldn't leave. Instead she willed cognizance into J.D., willed him *into* the Paused moment with her, until finally, with a popping sound of air rushing into an aluminum can as the seal was broken, he joined her in the space between seconds.

"Abby! What's happening? You were there, and you're here," his voice warbled frantically. It must be a shock for a non-Pauser to find themselves in the midst of a Pause. She wasn't even sure how it was possible. But she kept her connection with him, kept the contact of her hand on his arm as if it might be the only thing anchoring him to her. For all she knew, it was.

"No time to explain, and I'm not even sure I could. We have to get out of here."

She saw his training kick into survival mode, and he moved —limped really—with her back to the chopper. She touched her other hand to Siggy and willed him into the moment with them. It happened faster, easier this time. She wasn't sure if skill or necessity was driving this newfound attribute of her ability.

Siggy was noticeably more startled than J.D., but the Wolf overrode his clamoring and corralled him into line with them as they climbed into the chopper.

Siggy let go first as he moved to sit behind them, and as he broke physical contact he fell woodenly back into the freeze, clattering to the floor of the helicopter behind them. Abby winced, but J.D. just chuckled grimly, "He'll survive. Can you hold this much longer?"

"I don't think so," Abby exhaled an exhausted breath. Already the moment felt like it was fraying at the edges.

"Well, hold it as long as you can. At least until I get this thing started."

Abby nodded as sweat flecked on her forehead. She kept a hand on his shoulder, keeping him in the moment, as he fiddled and flipped at the controls, seemingly at random, with his one good arm. "Hurry, it's slipping," she said between gritted teeth.

Just as she felt the moment go, and time warp back into reality, the whirr of the chopper began as the blades slowly began to rotate above. There was a strange rebounding feel to reality as time snapped back. It was something Abby hadn't experienced the previous times. But then again, she'd never held it so long, or so intentionally before. Nor had she brought people in with her.

As time kick-started, a yell of pain sounded from the ground beneath the chopper. Abby had almost forgotten about the warlord and what she'd done to him.

"You Time Fighting, bitch! I'll kill you. I'll murder you, and your friends, and your family for this. I'll kill everyone you know!" The rest of his pained shrieks were lost beneath the gaining speed of the blades spinning above and the shouts of the men approaching the helicopter and their master.

Just as the men were about to reach the machine, J.D. raised the helicopter clumsily into the air, hands on the controls. It wobbled and dipped awkwardly, but it rose, just out of the reach of the men stopping beneath it. A few shots clinked off the exterior, but most of the surviving men seemed concentrated on their grievously wounded leader.

Abby watched as J.D. took them up into the night, looked out the passenger side door at the ground falling away beneath them, at the men tending to Alojz. Would he live? She wasn't sure. Her knife had bitten deeply.

Prague sprawled out beneath them. A few lights twinkled here and there around the fort, but farther out into the city was darkness, most people opting to conserve energy and resources.

"Goodbye, Prague," Siggy said sadly from behind them as he watched his home fall away. "Where to now?"

"I was thinking west," J.D. said, almost phrasing the

statement as a question, splitting the difference between them. "We need to get as far away from Alojz and his men as possible. New Central Europe is a long way from the other side of the Atlantic," he ended with a hopeful, questioning note in his voice.

"Alojz will be occupied for a time, I made sure of that," Abby grated out bleakly. J.D. nodded approvingly at her statement. "But west works for me. I wouldn't mind leaving this piss of a place behind me once and for all," she said.

"West," Siggy agreed.

They flew in silence, or at least as silent as something can be with the sound of the blades careening above. In time, J.D. opened his mouth again, looking at her out of the corner of his eye. "How long?"

Abby pulled her gaze away from where it had been blankly fixed on the dim landscape passing beneath. "Hmm?" Then she understood his question. "Oh. A minute maybe. I think—I don't really know."

J.D. nodded as Siggy whistled. "That's a long Pause."

"It is indeed," J.D. agreed with an impressed look on his face. They left it at that, for which Abby was glad. She didn't have answers to any questions they might have—how long, how she'd pulled them with her. It was all a mystery to her. But maybe, just maybe, she'd have the chance to find out now. Maybe she'd be safe—or at least as safe as a person could be in this broken world—with some actual friends around her.

"How long will we fly?" she asked her companion.

"Until the fuel runs out," J.D. indicated the light on the dash between them. "It won't get us as far as I'd hoped because it wasn't fully fueled up. Alojz probably had this relic as more of a badge of power and prestige than out of any real desire to use it regularly. Fuel is too hard to come by. But it'll do." He shrugged.

"It's better than any other option we had—will get us farther than anything else could have," Siggy said cheerfully somehow, despite all his injuries.

"It is at that," J.D. agreed and flashed a grin at the both of them, even as he winced in pain.

"You're hurt badly, aren't you?" she said worriedly.

He winced again. "If you can reach across and wrap my shoulder with something, I'll last until we land and can tend to it properly," he disagreed stoically.

Abby pulled off her jacket despite the cold and reached across to awkwardly bind him up with it as best as she could without disrupting his control of the aircraft. He mumbled a thanks as she sank back into her seat, arms pressed against her shoulders, hugging herself, fighting the pervading chill.

They flew all through the night until the grey of dawn lightened the horizon behind them.

They might be pursued, but Abby felt a lightness in her chest.

A new day. A new life. A new hope for the future.

———

**Don't miss out on your next favorite book!**
**Join the Melange Books mailing list at**
www.melange-books.com/mail.html

## THANK YOU FOR READING

Did you enjoy this book?

We invite you to leave a review at the website of your choice, such as Goodreads, Amazon, Barnes & Noble, etc.

## DID YOU KNOW THAT LEAVING A REVIEW...

- Helps other readers find books they may enjoy.
- Gives you a chance to let your voice be heard.
- Gives authors recognition for their hard work.
- Doesn't have to be long. A sentence or two about why you liked the book will do.

## ABOUT THE AUTHOR

Mathias Colwell grew up in far Northern California exploring redwood forests and cloudy beaches. He loves God, his family, and friends. Mathias has been a writer for most of his life, drafting his first stories as young as eight years of age. His desire to write fantasy was inspired by such authors as J.R.R. Tolkien, David Eddings and the late Robert Jordan. He is an avid traveler and all-around adventurer, having visited or lived in 27 countries. His travels have led him around the world to five continents including stays in Siberia, Spain, and Chile, and he attributes many of his passions and goals in life to these experiences. In his free time, he enjoys reading, outdoor activities such as soccer, snowboarding and water sports. Mathias has a passion for issues pertaining to social justice and human rights and hopes to influence these areas in the future.

mathiasgbcolwell.wixsite.com/author

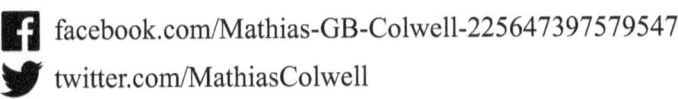

facebook.com/Mathias-GB-Colwell-225647397579547

twitter.com/MathiasColwell

## ALSO BY MATHIAS G.B. COLWELL
### WITH MELANGE BOOKS

**The Collector Series**

*The Collector*

*Blood Loss*

*Menagerie of Shadow*

*Reckoning and Retribution*

**Dark Arrow Trilogy**

*Dusk Runner*

*Entrance to Dark Harbor*

*Black Water Well*

**Novellas**

*An Age of Mist*

*A Burning Hope*